Ruling Out The What Ifs

- A Quarter Life Crisis

Table of Contents

Opening Chapter

Georgia sat in her small, one bedroom apartment, staring at the glow of her laptop screen. The cursor blinked on an empty document titled "Future Plans". The sound of the bustling city below drifted through her open window, a constant reminder of people's lives, moving on around her. At 25, she felt like she was standing still, trapped in the quicksand of her own making.

The apartment reflected her mind – cluttered and chaotic. Books she intended to read, lay in precarious stacks. Half-finished projects cluttered the desk and a vision board on the wall was filled with faded, unfulfilled dreams. The dreamcatcher her best friend Emma had gifted her, hung above her bed, looking out of place among the scattered clothes and unopened mail.

Georgia had always been the overachiever. In school, she was the straight-A-student, the one who excelled in every extracurricular activity, the one with grand plans and loads of friends. She graduated top of her class, pursued the 'perfect" college course, with plans to excel, make everyone proud and move to London with a vision of success that glittered like the skyline. But somewhere along the way. the sparkle dimmed.

Her phone buzzed, pulling her from her daydream. It was a text from her mother, asking if she was coming home for the family reunion next month. Georgia sighed and tossed the phone aside. Family reunions meant questions – questions about her job, her love life, her plans for the future. Questions she didn't have the answers to.

The truth was, Georgia was lost, confused, frustrated and excited all at once. Her job, once a source of pride, has become a monotonous cycle of pointless meetings and unfulfilled promises. The creative spark that once ignited her passion was buried under a mountain of spreadsheets and client demands. And her personal life? A series of dates that never went beyond the first, friendships that seemed to be fading as everyone moved forward, leaving her behind.

Georgia walked to the window and looked out at the city lights. Somewhere out there, people were living the lives she had dreamed of. They were making art, falling in love, starting families, and building empires. She felt an overwhelming sense of being an imposter in her own life, a life that had somehow veered off course.

Her mind wandered to the conversation she had with Emma just a week ago. Over coffee, Emma had just confessed her own doubts and fears. "It feels like everyone else has it all figured out" Emma said, stirring her matcha with a frown. "But the truth is none of us do. We're all just trying to make it through, one day at a time". Georgia nodded, feeling a brief sense of companionship. But now, in the solitude of her apartment, that companionship felt distant. She was alone with her thoughts, alone with the daunting realization that she was having what people called a "quarter-life-crisis".

She returned to her laptop and stared at the blank document. How did she even begin to outline her future, when the present felt so uncertain? Georgia's mind raced with possibilities, each one tinged with doubt. She thought of quitting her job and travelling the world, of going back to school, of starting her own business. But each idea was met with the same paralyzing fear; What if she failed?

The thought of failure loomed over her like a dark cloud, a constant reminder of the expectations she had set for herself, and the fear that she may never meet them. Georgia closed the laptop and sat back, feeling the weight of her decision settle over her.

In that moment, she made a promise to herself. She didn't have to have all the answers right now. She just needed to take it one step at a time, Maybe the path forward wasn't always about grand plans and ambitious goals. Maybe it was about small, deliberate choices.

Georgia took a deep breath and stood up. She walked over to her vision board and took down the faded pictures and quotes, replacing them with a single piece of paper. On it, she wrote "Find Joy in the Journey".

It was a small start, but it was something. As she pinned it to the board, she felt a flicker of hope. The road ahead was still uncertain, but for the first time in a long time, it felt like it may lead somewhere worthwhile

She sat back in her favourite, hot pink, office chair and pondered about where she was now, what she has done and what she still hopes to do, this is where she began....

Chapter 1: Who am I?

Who am I, such a broad question with everchanging answers, if you asked me that 5 years ago, I would say "Straight-A-Student, top of my class, confident, sexy, athletic and a great friend". But now, that the question is in front of me at this point in time, it fills me with anxiety instead of a confidence boost. My answers would be something along the lines of "lost, uninspired, lazy, lonely, single, introvert with crippling social anxiety". The same Georgia, who was the life of a party each weekend, just to be liked by everyone, is now a loner, who sits in each weekend binge watching the Gilmore Girls while still sleeping with her childhood teddy. Oh goodness, where do I even begin to find me again?

Ok, I need to think from a more positive light instead of focusing on all the negatives, I am a good friend, when I can be, but then again, I wasn't able to meet Emma that time she was really upset, because I was stuck in work, so can I still class myself as one? Oh no, this really isn't getting me anywhere!

I suppose I could say I'm hardworking, I excelled through school, battled through a college course I didn't even really like, and I work way over my paygrade at this new job, but once again this is the people pleaser in me.

I look at other people from my school year that skipped the college 'norm' and went travelling Asia, Australia and Canada and made friends for life, amazing memories and were able to be themselves and find who they really were. At least twice a day, I sit and think, have I missed all those amazing opportunities, do I regret jumping straight into the corporate world, renting a flat in a big city that is all go, go, go? Usually the answer is yes, but at the same time the people who travelled since school probably think the same thing, was it worth it as they've no work experience, no rental references and are "so behind" everyone else. And I think this sums up the quarter life crisis so well, no matter what you do, there's parts you may think you're missing out on or 'behind' in − on that note, who came up with that expression that you're "behind"? Behind who? Each person's life is their own, no one is behind anyone else, and everyone has a different timeline for life - that has always bothered me, but anyway, we move.

When I was younger, I thought I had it all planned out, good job, living in London with the love of my life, with 2 beautiful children, planning a wedding and a lot of amazing memories made all by 25. That has clearly changed, as I sat here in my Snoodie, single af with my cat as company. But I realize now that that's ok as there's plenty more time and I don't have to go by a general timeline, probably made by some man in a suit in the 60's, and 25-year-olds are only 7-year-old adults after all – that's my excuse anyway!

I have always adored the idea of travelling, seeing different cultures, meeting different people and stepping out of my comfort zone, but the guilt always lingered over me when it came to actually making a decision. My parents are growing older each day, do I really take that selfish leap and make memories while missing out on family time while it's still there? I worked so hard to make my way through college and my parents helped me big time with the fees that are involved in completing 4 years of misery. Is it selfish of me to pack up, travel for a year or two after all that hard work, possibly leading to me missing out on amazing work opportunities, I know my degree will always be there but each year there is also thousands of people fighting for the same jobs, with better experience, can I really sacrifice that?

Selfish is a word that popped up a lot during my thought process. Why? I don't really know, because deep down I know it's my life, it's short and I want to make some memories and find the real me. But as I touched on before, I am a people pleaser, and find it very hard to make decisions without thinking of everyone and everything it may affect. I never brought this up to my family or Emma, because I didn't want to face their reactions, which of course in my head, I was probably overthinking, but I could still never face it. In reality, Mom especially, always has my back in every decision I make and always wants the best for me, but I can't stand the heartbreak of moving so far away for possibly over a year! As of now, I'm only in London and she's in Edinburgh but yet it feels so far away on days like today when you just need a hug and a gentle "you'll be alright, you got this".

It's time to reinvent myself, I know who I want to become, so I just have to start acting like her, slowly I will become her! I imagined my dream 25-year-old self to be one of those Pilates girls that go for brunch with her girlfriends on a Sunday, dresses smart, walks confidently and is someone who has their shit together and always has something to look forward to! I already used to be confident in school and uni, so I know that confidence is deep down within me, I just have to find it.

Once again, like every January 1st, I began a list of everything I want to achieve, but this time it was different, I was determined to find me again, see what I enjoy and to see WHO I AM....

"Knowing yourself is the beginning of all wisdom" - Aristotle

Chapter 2: Finding Me

This is it, I finally made the decision, now it's time to stick to it and become a better person and most importantly, find Georgia again.

The first step for me was getting out of this Minion themed Snoodie that is probably well due a wash. Got changed, freshened up and walked my way to the pharmacy next door, I grabbed a facemask, foot mask, lip mask, hair mask and a bottle of bright pink nail polish – also saw something called a 'bum' mask – but let's leave that for another day, eh? I gathered my shopping and returned to my cluttered apartment; in order to feel relaxed, the apartment has to be clean right? I'm pretty sure I read something along the lines of "Clear Space, Clear Mind" in one of my self-help books that are currently still perched on my bookshelf, half read. Therefore, I threw on a "You're the Rich, Hot Aunt" playlist and danced around the apartment while clearing out all unnecessary shit that didn't benefit me or my life anymore. By the time it was clean, and my neighbours were probably scarred for life, watching my horrific dancing, I weirdly felt something within me, which I hadn't felt in a while, it was hope and excitement! I finally felt that something was going in the right direction, and I couldn't be happier.

I sat down, opened my shopping bag and let's just say by the time I had all the masks on me, I was glad I wasn't expecting any parcels, because boy would that postman be petrified of the sight that opens the door. But here I was, carefree, not planning 100 years in advance. Just being here and now, eating a bag of Magic Stars while shamelessly watching High School Musical. Something about childhood activities always manages to calm me down and allow me to switch off from 'adult' life.

I went to sleep that night with ease and with great hope for what was to come for me.

I woke the next morning to the usual alarm clock at 7:00am, a message from my boss saying I have a large assignment due today by 5pm, when realistically it would take 2 or 3 days. Already I woke up with stress, upset, anger and feeling like last night's hope and relaxation was just a dream. I spent all day typing up numbers and statistics and at that moment, I felt drained and once again uninspired. That is until I opened my phone to begin aimlessly scrolling once again and the first thing that popped up on my Instagram feed was "Just do it". This message is a common one which up until yesterday I would've disregarded, and it wouldn't have even registered in my brain, but for some reason, this time was different.

I felt strong, brave and inspired once again and in that moment of adrenaline......I pressed send on my email of resignation.

Oh my god, what have I done.

The good vibes of strength and courage were gone, and I just froze.

I'm 25, I'm supposed to have this stable job and continue to save for down the line, and I have just thrown it all away on a whim! I have rent, food, utilities, everything to pay for, and London is far from affordable!

I faceplanted onto my bed, grabbing 'Monk', my childhood teddy, for comfort. I then peeled my face from the covers after about 5 minutes of freaking out and just sat there. Usually at this time there would be nothing but panic running through my brain, but I decided to calm down, and feel what I was feeling, it's ok to feel panicked, scared, regretful but it's also ok to be excited and curious about what's to come.

Once I gathered myself, I rang Mom, I tried to tell her the news but couldn't get it out, the lump in my throat from crying and the snot running down my face (tmi I know but that's the reality!) made it impossible for me to string a sentence together. Mom realized something was wrong but couldn't work out exactly what, so she did what she does best, made me laugh, I eventually calmed down and surprisingly we ended up laughing at the situation and I was laughing at myself for being so upset.

The reassurance from Mom that it was the right idea, was everything I needed, and she was only delighted to hear I was coming home. She straight away started to make my bed, getting fresh PJs from Primark, a bottle of wine and a bag of Magic Stars, she knew me so well, even though I barely knew this new version of me, she still sees the little girl inside of me and knows how to comfort me.

I packed up my life in London and caught the Train to Edinburgh, I hadn't been home in over a year, Mom came to see me during the Summer in London, but I never came home, scared of all the questions and expectations that I'm smashing life in the 'Big City'. But here I was, walking through Waverley Station, hoping I wouldn't bump into someone I knew. Edinburgh is a big city, but it's still the type of place you'll see the same people, doing the same things and usually spot a neighbour on your travels. I made my way up the stairs to see my mom, waiting for me with open arms, all I wanted to do was run into her arms and cry but that lovely thing called social anxiety allowed me to bury my emotions until I reached the car.

Mom opened the door to the house where I was greeted by my 10-year-old 'puppy' Luna, completely in denial, she too was getting older while I was away living my own life. I spent the night in my new PJs cuddled up beside Mom and Luna, I went from laughing to crying to panic to complete bliss every couple of hours, feeling both relief I had quit and have time with Mom again with no stresses. To pure regret wondering what the hell I've done, moving into Moms house at 25 with absolutely nothing to show for my time in London, only an extra line on my CV.

Emma facetimed me just as I got into bed, we had said our goodbyes in London but this catch up had something so comforting about it, it was a reminder that I did come away from London with something, a best friend, your 20's are a tough time to make friends because all your school friends have moved away for college or are the other side of the world travelling, you may also have just drifted apart because of who you became as an adult outside of school. But Emma was a friend for life, I just knew it.

She was already making plans to come to Edinburgh to meet me and how she's always wanted to see the

Highland Cows and Edinburgh Castle, of which I forgot about the simplicity of the smaller things I've always taken for granted around here. We spent an hour talking about our feelings and the plans for her visit and by the end of the phone call, my regrets were fading away...

"Your vision will become clear only when you look into your heart. Who looks outside, dreams; Who looks inside, awakes" - Carl Jung

Chapter 3: Enjoying my own company

Now this was a new one for me, I always saw being by yourself as lonely, depressing and everyone viewed you as a loner. But I thought to myself, the person you spend the most time with is yourself, you better make it fun and like the person you are.

I began with the small things of trying new hobbies to see what I liked, went to Pilates, Pottery, Rock Climbing and everything in between, found a few I liked and a few I am glad I went to, because I know I wouldn't go again. Old me would class it as a waste of time if I didn't like something but this new mindset, I had allowed me to view it as "Ruling out the What Ifs".

Putting myself out there was one of the hardest obstacles to overcome, I was the girl that had a few drinks and could conquer the world but without them, I'd hide behind the group and be the last one to enter a room, hopefully unnoticed. Of course, all these new hobbies I've been trying kind of force you to go somewhere yourself, and yes even though you don't have a full conversation in the middle of a yoga pose, it still meant I was putting myself out there, which I was proud of myself for.

There it was, another positive feeling, finding its way back into my life, pride, I was proud of myself and I will continue to be proud of myself. Even if I fail, I still tried which is the main thing.

Then came the dreaded, "oh no, what will people be thinking?" phase, classes and hobbies are easy to blend into alone but when it came to simple things such as having lunch at a café, seeing your favourite movie at a cinema, these are the things we as humans are so scared to do, in case of other people's judgement. "Who cares what people think? They don't know me!" I'd remind myself every time I thought about stepping foot inside the café or cinema. But I finally did it, I grabbed a menu, chose the Pancakes with colourful candy floss toppings and the Pink Hot Chocolate with cream and marshmallows, my two favourite treats from my favourite café, Laila, in the Old Town of Edinburgh. I didn't read one word of book I was reading, because I was secretly having a private party inside, once again that sense of pride, I did it!!

Next on the list was the cinema, which was great timing because a movie came out that I was dying to see, but no one to go with me. In the past, I would've missed the movie because I wouldn't go myself, but this time I was determined. The cinema near my house was a nostalgic one, as I had spent so many years running in with excitement, smelling the popcorn in the air, collecting my kid's meal and sitting down beside Mom, who was just as excited to watch Paddington or Peter

Rabbit, yet coincidently always fell asleep half way through.

The second I walked through the doors, I was greeted by the staff and asked what movie I was here for, they didn't seem to bat an eyelid that I was there myself, maybe it is normal, maybe I was overthinking it all along. That salty smell of popcorn brought me right back to earth and my face lit up as I saw the kids boxes, I always used to get. Without my knowing, the cashier spotted me looking at the kids' box and says "We're all kids at heart, treat yourself!", little does she know she made my night. I happily walked towards the movie screen with my handful of popcorn, fruit shoot and a mini bag of Haribo's. I took my seat, settled in and realised, it's a cinema, literally no one can see me and everyone is focused on the movie, what was I so scared of all this time. Once again, I did it! It may sound so silly that a 25-year-old went to the movies and ate a kid's meal and gained so much joy and sense of achievement from it, but I didn't care, I was happy and that's all that mattered.

As I lay in my childhood bed with Monk, I realised we really are all kids at heart, pushed into the big bad world to fend for ourselves and all we need is some time to chill out, watch a cartoon, and be a kid again once and a while.

With all this new found confidence, I may have got over excited and booked my first trip, not very far, I was not that brave yet! I booked a weekend trip to Ireland, I have always wanted to go, plus it's only an hour away on a flight. I heard so much about Dublin, but I wanted to see what else Ireland had to offer, so I found County Kerry in the South of Ireland.

I arrived to Edinburgh Airport, waved goodbye to mom for the weekend and got on the escalator to go through security, of course it was the usual hustle and bustle of an airport. That mix of excitement, nervousness and sadness, people travelling for many different reasons, it's kinda strange if you think about it, one person's flight would be for a holiday of a lifetime and the passenger next to them could be flying home to mourn the loss of a loved one, you never really know what's going on in people's lives, eh?

As we approached the runway, the nerves hit, once again that feeling of regret and what ifs started running through my mind. But I remembered, I made a decision to "rule out the what ifs". I put my big girl pants on and knew there was no going back now! After a smooth flight and what everyone knows as a "Ryanair" landing, I arrived into Cork Airport, a small airport, but it was ideal as I was so overcome with emotion, both good and bad, I didn't want all the fuss of navigating an airport.

Cork was the closest airport to County Kerry, one quick bus trip to Killarney and I had arrived! Killarney was beautiful, its scenery was amazing and a place that had everything, shops, nightlife and nature. I checked into my hotel, overlooking the breathtaking mountains and lakes, sat on the balcony and checked in with myself. You see so many people on Instagram nowadays with their airport outfits, weekends in Dubai, getting engaged in Paris while little 'ol me was so happy to be sitting in the countryside on a trip that cost me £200 in leggings and a hoodie from Primark.

With that I found myself, knocking myself down, thinking things like "you're broke, unemployed and have a little trip to Ireland and think you're on top of the world!?". Once again, I was back to feeling depressed and just sick of this life I was living, feeling like I was getting nowhere! "Will I just get a job as a waitress in a café in Edinburgh, live with mom until I save up and then book that ticket to Australia, like everyone else my age is doing?" I thought to myself. When in reality, that's not what I wanted, yes, Australia looks amazing but I like Europe, I love being close to my family and I didn't just want to go with the 'norm'. I did that with college and it wasn't even something I wanted, yet it led me to sit here paying off student loans with a job I just packed in, and probably won't get another opportunity like that again. I sat in the hotel room all of the first day crying, stressing and didn't know what to do.

After ordering room service, I peeled myself out of bed to go and explore Killarney while I was there. I visited the National Park and brought myself to the local shopping centre just to look around, people watch and have some time to think.

The next day, I woke up, with the idea I was going to make the most of this trip that I was originally so excited for. Just down the road from my hotel there was a place called Torc Waterfall. I sat by the waterfall for about an hour and whilst there I realised; I was doing exactly what I said I hated. I was comparing myself to these super slim, influencers online with their amazing sponsored getaways and picture-perfect relationships. I am not them and they are not me, I have my own life path and that isn't one I would like to be on personally, so why would I compare myself to someone I wouldn't swap places with?!

I was up for a challenge, wanted to clear my head and get back that sense of achievement and courage I felt when I quit my job, so I looked around, saw a sign saying 'Cardiac Hill', which in itself sounded scary, but I got up off the wet rocks, with my damp ass, tied my hoodie around my waist and began the walk. On the way up I felt every emotion possible, the fear of failing again, joy, courage, sadness, achievement, all of which are so normal to experience when you're challenging yourself, especially doing something new! Surprisingly, once I reached the top, I was the most alive I've felt in a long time! Once again, I sat down at the top with my packed lunch (PS the Irish don't lie when they go on about how great Tayto Sandwiches are!), took a picture, but most of all reflected on how one decision I made at the bottom of the hill, changed my day for the better.

I made my way back on the bus to Cork Airport, boarded my flight and arrived into Edinburgh. Mom was of course waiting for me with open arms once again, this i loved, because when I went away when I was living in London, I'd come home to an empty apartment but with Mom there, I could tell her all my adventures, the highs the lows, everything! That one little solo trip to Ireland, may have changed my life. I learned amazing life lessons and fell in love with a town, that's so close to my hometown that I can visit when I'm feeling low and need that kick up the bum again!

I printed out the picture I took on the top of Cardiac Hill and hung it above my bed to remind myself each day, you can make a quick decision that can change your life for the best!

"I never found a companion that was so companionable as solitude"

- Henry David Thoreau

Chapter 4: Reality

The joys of adult life hit hard once I saw my London savings, dwindling away bit by bit every day. I realised I had to get up and find some source of income to fund whatever it was, that was going to be my next adventure. I got to the horrible task of summarizing your life onto an A4 piece of paper to hand to strangers, in hopes to receive a job to get me by.

I did have a bit of a breakdown after this day, full of upset and regrets for leaving a job I worked so hard to get a qualification for, with good money, fast forward to now I am back to living with Mom, applying to work for minimum wage jobs I have no interest in. I don't think I was too hard on myself this time; I knew these feelings were valid so I allowed myself to sit with them and comfort myself while I cried. But then again, I had to pick myself up, accept what I was given and try remind myself it is all the journey that will lead me to where I am meant to be.

I got offered a job in a local café, weekdays, laid back, chatting to customers, making friends with my new colleagues, all in all it wasn't as bad as I expected. I worked during the day, planning new ideas in the evenings. Enjoying dinner with Mom, each evening, having chats about our day. I missed that, so in a way I am glad to be back to experience that before I move onto the next chapter of my life.

After all my evenings of planning, I discovered, I had a pull to Asia, a country full of different cultures, many ways of life and people from so many different backgrounds. I researched it a lot, hopeful I would eventually get there, but it was daunting seeing how big it really was and the price of transport and accommodation just kept adding up. I realised my job in the café was not gonna cut it! I applied for some weekend jobs in the local bars and nightclubs, I wasn't a drinker so 'missing out' on a Saturday night because I was working, didn't bother me! Slowly but surely, I saved enough to book my flights to Thailand.

I did it without thinking, after months of planning and discussing it with Mom and Emma, I was just so ready (or so I thought).

I had 5 months left. Before I leave. By myself. Half way across the world. AM I CRAZY?!?!?!

The plan sounded amazing in theory, but when it was booked, I never felt so unsure about something before. Something didn't feel right. Mom assured me it was just panic of doing something new, but not this time, I never had this feeling, something wasn't right.

I rang Emma for advice, she listened to me cry, hyperventilate and freak out but even with all that, she just listened, said exactly what I needed to calm down and then spoke about options. We spoke about everything from cancelling to just winging it but eventually came to a middle ground. Emma had spotted a group trip being held by a girl she followed on Instagram, around the same time I was supposed to go, so she recommended, maybe I book in for the group trip for the first 2 weeks until I get the lay of the land and then I can go out on my own once I'm comfortable, and who knows, one of the people on the trip may have the exact same plan!

The next 3 months I worked my ass off to save for this trip, I had already been home 6 months and I needed something new, something exciting!

"Face reality as it is, not as it was or as you wish it to be"

- Jack Welsh

Chapter 5: Girl Time

The time finally came for Emma to come and see me! I missed that girl so much but thank God for Facetime, I'd be lost without our daily call where we just offload everything, have each other on the phone while we do our makeup, clean our rooms, showering, during our hot girl walk, as long as we have each other on the phone, we don't have to be speaking, just knowing the company is there, it really helps! She arrived on a Friday morning and was spending the week here! I caught the tram to Waverley Station, eagerly awaiting her arrival. We had been planning this for months!

As soon as I saw her long, ginger hair through the crowd, I immediately lit up with happiness and started running towards her (tripping on multiple suitcase wheels on the way may I add) but so worth it. Emma has saved me so many times, I only met her when I moved to London, she was working in the same company as me and showed me around on my first day. From that day on she has been there through all my highs and lows, held me when I was ghosted after a date, let me crash at hers when I got homesick and celebrated with me each year on my Birthday, I could always count on her!

We skipped out of the train station and as we exited, Emma got to see Edinburgh Castle in all its beauty! "This is right in the middle of town? You walk past this every day?" she squealed with excitement. This made me realize, I need to live in the moment and realise what's around me in this beautiful part of the world! We had the whole week planned out; we are both 'serial planners' so we loved comprising an itinerary while on Facetime. I had to introduce her to my favourite café, Laila, with the pink hot chocolate and candy floss pancakes, but once we got there, I realized how different this was to when I first got back home. I cried coming out of the train station, nervously entered the café by myself and now I am skipping around with my best friend, showing her the beauty of my hometown!

We sat for hours chatting all things life and then continued on up the Royal Mile to the Castle, climbed Carlton Hill overlooking the city and had the best day ever. Once we got home, Mom had already set up my room for the two of us, I had my two favourite women that I look up to most, beside me and I couldn't be happier!

With Emma, I could be my most authentic self, I showed her all my Thailand plans, where I worked, where I used to go to school, Luna and most importantly, Monk, who I think made a first great impression!

We went to bed, giggling like children, staying up watching movies, eating popcorn and just being ourselves. Excited for what was to come the next day!

We had planned to do the NC500, which is one of
Scotland's most iconic road trips up the North Coast,
the route started in Inverness, about 3 hours away from
home, so we woke early, made some more pancakes and
Mom dropped us to the caravan rental centre. We
collected a bright pink Volkswagen camper, stocked up
in Tesco and made our way up the road. Emma had
compiled all of our favourite songs onto a playlist so we
sang the whole way to the first stop, we explored each
site, around Inverness, up to Thurso, over towards Ben
Nevis Mountain and back around to Glencoe and
eventually into Edinburgh. The trip took us 5 days but
it was the best 5 days ever, we just sang, talked, ate,
danced in the rain, swam in the sea, laughed, cried,
hiked, it was just perfect in every way and it was so
needed!

We arrived home once again, Emma was due to leave
the next day so we treated ourselves to some cocktails
overlooking the castle and went home to watch High
School Musical, which once again turned into a karaoke
night! It was bittersweet the next morning, we had such
a great time we didn't want it to end, but it was time to
get back to reality and continue our adult lives until we
met again. Emma was already planning to come back
for the Christmas Markets so I knew it wouldn't be too
long! We said our emotional goodbyes and I got back to
work that afternoon.

"Girl time is sacred. It is where we get to recharge, rejuvenate and remind ourselves that we are stronger together"

Chapter 6 – The Leap

Here it was, the day I was most fearful of, yet it was also the day I was looking forward to the last 6 months. Todays the day I go to the airport with a 20kg bag (learned the hard way this was unnecessary) and a heart full of dreams. Mom woke me up at 3am for my 7am flight but I didn't sleep at all that night so I was wide awake when she came in. We sat on my bed, talking about how amazing it'll be and how she's only a call away. I think Mom was low key trying to tell herself it will be fine too.

I added the last few things to my already overweight bag. Monk & my phone charger were the last to be packed, but then I was physically ready, mentally not so much. We arrived at the departures hall, once again, that dreaded wave goodbye when you step onto the escalator to security. I immediately went into the bathroom before security and quietly bawled my eyes out for a few minutes, before cleaning myself up, popping in some earphones and drinking my last Irn Bru for a while. While scrolling TikTok, I came across this video that says "I have no idea what I am gonna do tomorrow.....how exciting!" which kind of gave me a sense of excitement instead of my nerves. But once again it is so natural to be nervous and excited and everything in between, this was such a big change!

I heard my gate being called for boarding and immediately, I felt sick. It hit me, this is real, what am I doing?! Once again, the joys of doubt and fear and regret took over but I did it anyway. I showed my passport of my 18-year-old self, took my seat on the plane and took a moment to just look at the picture of myself, 18, the years they say you have it all. All I could feel it pity for that girl looking back at me, she was so scared, stressed, anxious about college and London and leaving her friends. I would love to go back and hold her and tell her how she meets the amazing Emma, falls in and out of love a few times, has enough strength to quit her job and find a new her. But this then brought me back to the now, that 18-year-old fought so hard to get me exactly where I was now, I fought so hard for me, I made that scary decision to leave everything and focus on me and now here I am, a few months and mental breakdowns later, I made it, I got through it and I am off to create some amazing memories to last a lifetime!

We sat on the runway, waiting for take-off, trying to pick what movies to watch for the next 7 hours of flying. I thought about a generic movie that would look appropriate to watch on a plane and then thought, nope, I need my comfort movies right now, so Hannah Montana, you're up! I sat back with my pink neck pillow around my neck, singing along to Miley in my head and eventually got startled by the air hostess asking what I'd like for breakfast, I went for a soggy looking ham and cheese croissant, tea and a muffin, not exactly the luxury of a first-class Scottish Fry, but it did its job. I usually hate pretzels also, but I munched on those tiny little bags you get for free, the whole way to Bangkok, purely because they were free, and what girl doesn't like free snacks?!

Touch down in Bangkok, blast of hot air hits me, we shuffle down the stairs into the terminal where I no longer get greeted with "Welcome Home, Georgia" by the immigration officer, it's all paperwork and visas and that feeling like you've done something wrong even though you 100% haven't. I walked through the arrival gates to see a Thai man holding a sign "Georgia Williams", he welcomed me to Thailand and ushered me to the group accommodation. I arrived to see about 10 girls and 10 guys all hanging out by the pool of our hostel, I, on the other hand, ran to my room and bawled my eyes out once again. So, I cleaned myself up for the 3rd time today and made my way downstairs for dinner with the group, the usual horrible icebreakers began "My name is Georgia, I am a ......" I just went blank.

What am I? Who am I?

"....ammmm I'm a 20 odd year old wanting to find herself somewhere around the world". There, I said it, it was out there, now they know what a sad case I am, brilliant, there goes my chances of gaining any friends here. To my surprise they turn around all at once and say "Like all of us so!" laughing. Oh my god, I'm not alone, I'm not a sad case, most people in their 20's are in the same boat as me!

We spent the night laughing and playing and then we all went to bed after the long day of travel.

The next day, we woke to the sounds of someone's FaceTime ringtone, a mom that forgot the time difference between the UK and Thailand! We gathered in the kitchen, found out a bit more about each other and looking at our plans for the day. Me and this other girl, Megan from Ireland, who share the same bunk, got talking, we both were in the same situation, first trip far from home and we were able to lean on each other for support when it got tough. It's funny how people are jealous of the things you try escape from, for example Megan was dreaming of a good job in London, but she had a boyfriend back home who didn't want to leave and she was scared to lose him while following her own dreams. She couldn't believe, I left the great job and lovely apartment but at the same time she applauded me for taking the risk and going on the journey to find me. Somehow, I think we are all going to inspire each other on this trip.

As much as I loved talking to Megan, I know it was good to mingle and meet everyone else in the group, so we split up, joined the rest of the group and set off for the day, first stop, the city of Bangkok! We all got our Tuk-tuks into town, visited a few amazing temples and eventually arrived to Icon Siam, had a walk around the designer shops and the indoor floating food market. Seeing the diversity of people in the shopping centre was amazing, from working class people working their family food stalls, to the top of the top buying a Porsche and some Gucci T-shirts. We tried some new foods which were amazing and got some pictures on the rooftop! I watched a TikTok about a 'secret' rooftop door behind a Starbucks on the top floor and led everyone to it, my crazy planning, pays off sometimes after all!

Once we returned to the hostel again, we sat down, played a few more games and that's when I met Jason. I know, I know, everyone says not to have a 'holiday romance' so I had my guard up to begin with. Jason was from Glasgow, 1 hour drive from my house back in Edinburgh, small world, eh? He was tall, dark and handsome and to be honest, I spotted him on my first evening but first thing that came to mind was a major fuckboy so I steered clear, or so I thought! Jason came over to me with a drink that night, to which I declined as this new journey I'm on is a sober one, I never had a problem with alcohol, but I'd rather spend the money on making memories and bettering myself nowadays. Anyway, back to Jason, surprisingly, that drink I declined was a non-alcoholic gin and tonic, he too had the same idea as me. We chatted about life, a bit about our past and how we ended up in Thailand. Before we knew it, it was bedtime. I went to bed that night, smiling like a child and knew I was fucked there and then.

My guard clearly didn't stay up very long as the next morning, who decided to bring me my iced coffee.... only Jason of course! In an attempt to steer him off course, I introduced him to my new friend Megan and continued on with our day! Next stop, Phi Phi Islands!

The islands have been on my bucket list since I was 16, but of course I was focusing so much on school and my career I was ok with missing out on it. I realised, I made the right decision back in London, less than a year later and I'm sitting on a ferry on the way to *the* Phi Phi Islands with a group of amazing people who are all on similar journeys!

Amongst all this excitement and being overwhelmed with emotion upon seeing the turquoise water and amazing islands, I realised, I'm not too good with boats. A burst of nausea came over me and I couldn't get to the side of the ship quicker!

While I'm puking my guts up over the side of the boat into the fish filled, clear ocean, hair all over the place, Jason decides to check up on me - this surely turned him off me - but no, he made sure I had water and sat with me until we docked. I wished he would stop being so sweet I really didn't need this, I was focusing on myself!!

Anyway, we arrived on solid ground (thank god!), walked the length of the golden sandy beaches with long tail boats lining the shoreline, restaurants along the beach and signs for tonight's fire show! Checked into our villas for the night and oh my god I was in love with the place, I wanted to FaceTime Mom and Emma and show them the place but their world is still spinning too, they're in work or asleep whenever I go to call and that was tough, homesickness finally hit. I think this was the case for a lot of us as we spent the evening sitting on the beanbags on the beach, chatting and comforting each other. We decided to give the nights fire show a miss and rescheduled for the following night. It was nice we were all in the same situation, we were able to lean on and understand each others emotions.

The next morning, we woke to fruit salad on the balcony, prepared by the lovely locals. We started the day with a longtail boat tour (I remembered my sea sickness pills this time), it was amazing, indescribable beauty. We snorkelled with the fish, visited Maya Bay and the Monkey Beach, all memories I would treasure forever. Megan, Jason and I, sat together on the boat back to the island, talking the whole way back about how amazing the day was and how we couldn't wait for the fire show, that was until the tiny boat decided to breakdown in the middle of the sea for 2hrs, at this point the pills didn't help the seasickness at all and I was puking overboard again in front of everyone. You guessed right, Jason came to save the day again with water and holding my sopping wet hair back while I embarrassed myself for the 2nd time in 3 days!

Boat fixed, we returned to the island, got freshened up and changed for the night. I could feel my confidence creeping back in tonight and I had butterflies in my stomach, like I was actually on the right path this time and finding the real Georgia! With this new confidence building, I wore a dress I brought with me that's been sitting in the back of my wardrobe for years, I was keeping it for a special occasion. That day, I realised two things: 1) Wear the damn dress, you never know when your last day is going to be 2) That day was a special occasion in my own head, it may be silly to others but to me, I found my confidence again and that was major for me!

I threw on a floor length, red dress with a plunged neckline, checked myself out a few times and for the first time in years, left for the night without having a thousand mental breakdowns because I have a pouch at the base of my belly and "nothing looked good". I

42

posted the picture on my Instagram story, of course my
hype girl Emma came through saying she could see a
new sexy, confident Georgia shining through. This gave
me more reassurance I was doing the right thing! As
Megan and I approached the reception to meet the rest
of the group before the fire show, we bumped into
Jason, who was looking quite handsome with his
oversized, white shirt, left open and his casual beach
shorts. That night was about me, making more friends
and enjoying the once in a lifetime opportunity to see a
fire show for the first time on a beach in the Phi Phi
Islands, so Jason was pushed out of my mind for as long
as possible.

I've had my fair share of dates leading to nothing,
catching feelings and being ghosted so I was weary of
anything male related at that point. The main thing
was, I needed to love myself first before exploring any
other connections.

We sat and watched the show, it exceeded expectations,
a breathtaking display of talent by the locals and there
was an amazing vibe for the night. It turned midnight,
some of the group had gone to bed so it was a few
other people from our group remaining and Jason & I
were sat on the edge of the shoreline just soaking up
the good vibes. Then it happened, Jason reached out his
hand and placed it on mine, I got butterflies straight
away, a feeling I haven't experienced with anyone

before, but Georgia comes first. I had a chat with him explaining my mission while travelling and that I just couldn't risk all my progress for a boy I've just met. He respected my decision thankfully and there was no awkwardness, just a chatty stroll home along the beach and we split up to go to our Villas for the night.

The days after the show were amazing, walking the island, visiting the viewpoints and enjoying some amazing food! Then it was time to leave, next stop Phuket! We arrived to our new hostel, definitely a shocker coming from our own villa to another hostel with 12 beds in each dorm, but it was all part of the experience I suppose! It made us all grow closer and I made some amazing friends in the last few days. I finally called Mom, she was doing great, following my travels on my Instagram stories and she explained how proud of me she was for chasing my dreams and could see I was glowing! I spoke to her for an hour, filling her in on every detail, wishing she was there with me (I may have left Jason out of the stories), I couldn't deal with the questions, the lectures or whatever her reaction would be, all that matters is she was happy, I was happy and Luna is still roaming around the place.

The final day came, we were all speaking about our plans for the remainder of our travels, most were going home, some of us were splitting up and continuing to Bali and Vietnam. We said our goodbyes the next morning and all went our separate ways, or so I thought, I was in the queue in Bangkok airport to board the flight to Bali, I was terrified of doing this alone but knew it had to be done if I wanted to continue this work on myself. I may have had another cry in the bathrooms before we boarded, but once again, tidied myself up and got on the plane. I sat down in my assigned seat, popped my Air Pods in and settled in for the flight. In between podcast episodes, I hear a familiar accent, a Scottish accent, on a flight to a small island in Asia? It couldn't be! Oh my god, it was.....

Jason was sitting right behind me.

I continued on listening to my podcasts I downloaded before the flight. I wiggled around on the seat, holding in the urge to pee for ages just to avoid having to walk towards him down the aisle. One hour in and I can't hold it anymore, I get up, flick up my hood and walk as quick as I can to the toilets, on my return I kept my head down and shuffled into my seat, undetected. Ok, maybe I wasn't so sleek, because I felt 2 hands on my shoulders, I looked up to see Jason looking down at me, "Hey stranger!" He smiled, "Fancy seeing you here!".

"Oh my god hi!!" I said enthusiastically, while dying on the inside, but at the same time, it was nice to know I wasn't completely alone over here. But he doesn't have to know that.

I arrived into Bali Terminal, got greeted by my driver, parted ways with Jason and arrived to my villa. I got an amazing, private villa in Ubud with my own pool for only £30 per night, I couldn't believe it, this was a dream!! "Isn't this amazing Mo-". Oh, that was the tough part of solo travel, you see the most amazing things and you turn to tell someone and no one is there to listen.

I had 2 bags of Tayto in my bag that I had brought with me from my trip to Ireland, both for safe keeping, but I opened a packet, sat by the pool and just reflected for the day.

I am here, I did it, all by myself!

I spent the next few days, journalling my adventures, visiting Temples, getting blessed in the holy water temple and had a monkey sit on my shoulder in the Monkey Forest! Weirdly, I didn't feel too homesick this time. But this came with a bit of shame once again, Emma was working in London, Mom was still doing her daily tasks in Edinburgh and here I was living it up and they barely came into my mind. Am I really that horrible?? That moment, I received a text from Jason "Hey girl, feeling kinda homesick today, would love a friendly chat if you're keen?". How could I say No? He was there for me and to be honest I could do with a chat right now too.

We arranged a time and place and met at the local beach for sunset.

Bali sunsets were just amazing, they cheered me up every evening and I was excited to see the sunrise, over the rice fields the next morning.

We caught up, filled each other in on our adventures so far and then came the tears and hugs we both needed. Surprisingly at the end of it, I actually I said what I needed to say and I felt so much better going to bed that night. We caught a moped back to my place; he walked me to the door and went back on his way to his own accommodation. As my eyes were closing for the night, my phone buzzed and lit up the room, "Emma?" I thought, reaching for the phone. Nope, it was Jason

"Thanks for tonight, it really helped G, I couldn't bring myself to say it to you, but I fly home to Glasgow in the morning. I really do hope we can catch up sometime - here's my Instagram, chat soon x"

Immediately, I started crying, I'm officially here myself, we never said our proper goodbyes! I cried myself to sleep with intentions of messaging him in the morning and maybe doing an Instagram snoop.

I woke up feeling lonely, but excited, today was my last day here until I fly back to London to surprise Emma! I had booked the return to London, just to see her, I couldn't wait to tell her all my news, I didn't hear from

47

her much this week either so I wanted to check up and see how she was!

I spent my last day, strolling around the streets, went to a healer for a session; this was amazing! And then I made my way back to Seminyak to my hotel. I checked in, went to the spa for a £5 massage and fell asleep before I could even have dinner. It was needed though, with a 3am wakeup call arranged, I peeled myself out of bed, still fully dressed, and made my way out the door and into the taxi.

Arriving at the departure gates, I pushed my way through security, made it to my gate which wasn't boarding for another 2 hours, Bali airport was a lot smaller than anticipated. Still half asleep, I went for a nap and set an alarm for boarding time. When I woke, I text Mom to let her know the flight number, she loved tracking the flights, I told her I loved her and I couldn't wait to see her! I boarded the flight, set up my movies and was on my way home!

"You don't
have to see
the whole
staircase, just
take the first
step"

Chapter 7 - Lost

I landed into London, caught the familiar underground to Emma's flat, I was so excited to hug her and tell her everything!!

I ran up to her door, knocked, but no answer. It's a Tuesday, she works from home now, where could she be?

I rang her, I was going to pretend I was still in Bali, then the surprise wouldn't be ruined, I thought. The phone rang out.

I made my way back to Trafalgar Square, sat down near my old office, thought about how far I came since I lived here and just waited to hear from Emma. An hour went by, finally, a text from Em! "Hey girl, what's up?". I rang her as soon as it came through, she finally answered, "Where are you, I've come to London to see you!" The surprise was over but I just couldn't contain my excitement! "Oh" she said, "I'm in Jakes for the week". Jake?! Who the hell was Jake? And why doesn't she seem excited? "Girl, you have so much to tell me, where can we meet?" I said, hiding my confusion and upset.

"G, I'm busy ok, I'll call you when I'm free!" She said before hanging up the call.

What is wrong with her, I thought to myself. I'm back, we haven't seen each other in ages and she's "too busy" she won't even come and see me after I fly to London to surprise her?

I run into the public bathrooms, cry my eyes out before ringing Mom, I told her what happened and she told me to come home and reassess from there.

So, I did, I caught the same train I left London on a year previous, and made my way back to Edinburgh. While on the train, I spotted the text from Jason with his Instagram handle. I had nothing else to do to pass the time so I had a snoop. I knew it! His profile picture was him and another girl, a model looking girl, may I add.

I'm so glad I kept my guard up; he only wanted a holiday romance and that's it! Typical boys! I tried to keep a brave face and seem unbothered by it, but I may have had to wipe a tear or two.

I finally arrived into Edinburgh, welcomed home by Mom, I could always count on her to make me feel at home straight away. We spent the night going through my photos and telling stories about our adventures the last couple of weeks. The next day, I walked into town and really sat and appreciated the beauty of Edinburgh. The castle was looking amazing on this sunny day so I snapped a picture, put it on my Instagram stories and continued up the hill to Laila, "the usual?" The waitress grinned. "Yes please" I laughed! It was bittersweet, the

51

idea of home where it's so normal, nothing has changed and I just continue on like nothing has happened. She arrived with my Pancakes and Hot Chocolate and commented "well that's not a Scottish tan and I haven't seen you in a while, were you abroad?". It was quiet so she pulled up a chair and asked me all about my travels. Something was so comforting, telling a complete stranger all the ups and downs of travel. As I finished storytelling, I thought to myself, I came in here, ordered, sat down at the table by myself and spoke to someone new, all without even thinking of my anxiety or nerves. Maybe this trip really has changed my life!

As I left the cafe, my phone rang, hopeful it was Emma, I answered it without thinking. "Hey G" came from the end of the phone in a Scottish accent. "Oh no", I thought, why did I answer!! "Hey Jason!" I said with a shaky voice. "I see you're finally home, why didn't you tell me!" He said. I paused, not knowing whether to bring up the girl on his Instagram yet, but I decided not to for now. "I was literally just about you text you!" I lied. "I'm currently on the train to Edinburgh right now, see you in an hour?" He said excitedly. "Sure!"

I ran home as quick as I could, changed out of my million layers of clothes I was wearing to adjust to the freezing temperatures of Scotland! Mom spotted me as I was leaving, "going somewhere nice, eh?" She grinned, it's like she can read my mind! I laughed as I left the house, trying to avoid the awkwardness. I walked to Waverley Station once again, there he was, walking towards me, "he looks different with clothes on" I thought, and not in that way weirdo!

His face lit up as he walked towards me, as he threw his arms around me, I felt those stupid butterflies again. This was wrong, I had to ask him about that girl soon. We walked through the city and sat in the Gardens, "there's something so beautiful about this city, and it's not just the scenery" he grinned. I laughed it off, started talking about our adventures and how we were feeling. Like it was telepathy we both said "I feel so lost since I'm back", we paused looked at each other and burst out laughing. "We are quite literally the same person G, I love it!" He said. We spoke more about feeling lost, like something's missing. I have heard people say that though, once you travel, you leave a piece of you in each country you visit, when you return you rarely feel whole. We laughed and cried for hours just watching the world go by in front of us. I loved that he wasn't afraid to express how he felt, he didn't feel like he had to put on a show with me and I was the same.

Now was my chance, how do I approach this without coming on too heavy? "Sooo, that girl in your Instagram picture is stunning, you're a lucky man", oh god, I regret saying it the moment it left my lips. He burst out laughing! My soul left my body with embarrassment, and I didn't even hear the answer yet. "You mean my sister, yeah the looks run in the family, eh?". A smile grew on my face unknowingly, giving him his clarification that I'm interested and relieved it wasn't his girlfriend. What have I done!! He could see by my reaction I needed to change topic of conversation so he asked if I was hungry and would like to grab something to eat. Even though I had just eaten a whole stack of pancakes, loaded with candy floss, I agreed. I loved spending time with him, he was warm, felt like home and we really were the same person, I finally felt like I could just be me!

After the meal, he insisted he walked me home. Dreading the possibility of him and Mom meeting, I waited until I got just around the corner from my house and ushered him to the train so he wouldn't miss it. Just as I told him the time and said bye, he grabbed my waist pulled me in and kissed me. The butterflies in my stomach grew, I had been wanting to kiss this man for weeks now and it finally happened!

He smiled, pulled away and ran to catch his train. Me on the other hand was a little a giddy little girl, I skipped into the house smiling from ear to ear! I went straight to my room and just lay there and soaked up this amazing feeling!

Everything was coming together, at last! Yes, I feel a bit lost being home but when I'm with him, I feel complete. But I do know that this year was for working on me, so I still have to spend time with me, and continue to enjoy my own company even if Jason does enter the equation full time.

I was awoken from my daydream by my phone calling, it was Emma. I was no longer excited to see her name appear on my phone. The girl, I've been through my adult milestones with, wouldn't leave her new boyfriend to come and welcome me home after travelling. She hasn't checked up on me in over 2 weeks.

I let the phone ring out, then did exactly what she did, one hour later I text "What's up?", she replied with another phone call, so I answered. "Hey" I said unenthusiastically. "Hey girl, what's up with you? You seem off?" She replied in a giddy voice, as if none of this just happened. "What's wrong?!" I exclaimed, "I just spent the last 3 weeks across the world, finding myself and finding new confidence and more friends and you couldn't even come to see me when I came direct to London to surprise you?!". Here it was, the sentence that broke our friendship "Ok Georgia, yeah you're great, you quit everything like the careless adult you are, went back to your shitty hometown, working a shitty job and spent most your savings on a 3 week holiday, then expect everyone to drop everything and come and see you when you decide to come back?!" I just hung up, I couldn't believe it, she was jealous.

She is stuck in the rat race of London, with her one-night stands, being overworked and has every penny she makes in a savings account but has made no special memories, while I had the balls to quit and do what would make me happy. I didn't expect Emma to be like that, I thought she'd support me through everything. Yet another friendship lost to comparing other people's lives to yours and being jealous of someone instead of being proud.

I sat in my bed stuck between shocked and upset, Mom came in, I told her what happened and she just sat with me for a while, "it's her loss not yours Georgia, remember that", the most typical Mom sentence, was actually exactly what I needed to hear at the time.

Once again, I felt lost, absolutely no friends anymore, I was back working at a job I didn't want to be at, sleeping in my childhood room and all the depression just hit me like a truck.

I needed comfort, I needed to get away from home for the day so I rang Jay, booked the next train to Glasgow and gave him the biggest hug once I saw him. He felt like home to me. We hadn't seen each other since the kiss, this time was so different there was no awkwardness, no beating around the bush, just open conversations that led to every possible emotion and well needed cuddles.

We spoke about us, what was happening between us and how we both felt about it. We decided to take things slow as we were both on the same journey of finding ourselves and loving ourselves first. We continued to talk and walk for the day before I had to board my train home. We said our goodbyes before we got to the platform and I walked away the next part felt like a movie, he once again ran up to me, grabbed my hand, pulled me close and kissed me. It was like just him and I existed in this moment. This was it; I can feel it. I reluctantly said goodbye again before taking my seat on the train home. The second we departed the station, I receive a text "See you soon G, together we're never lost, I hope to spend life together crossing out the What Ifs". Yes, I know, it all sounded a bit cheesy. But I loved it, I loved him! He remembered my purpose of 'crossing out the What Ifs" and I felt ready to take the leap and cross out the what ifs with him!

"Not until we are lost do we begin to understand ourselves"

- Henry David Thoreau

Chapter 8 - Love Bubble

Yes, ok, I may have been in a love bubble. I found someone when I wasn't looking for them and immediately hit it off.

It's funny, I spent so many years on dating apps, posting the best pictures of me, all my best qualities and leaving out every detail that was actually me. But then I manage to pull a gorgeous guy when I'm getting sick over a boat, hair up in a mess, wearing 3 day clothes and crying. The world works in mysterious ways, eh?

Jason was my home, he was like my comfort blanket, anytime we met it was so peaceful, my brain went quiet and I just soaked up the moments we were together.

We had similar childhoods, a single mom doing 99% of the work and a dad who showed up the odd time to bring us to the park for the day. He had a twin sister; I am an only child so it was nice having her around too!

He arrived in Edinburgh after 6 weeks of us talking, it was finally time to meet Mom. I don't know why I was so nervous, he was great, she's great and they would get along perfectly but I think those nerves are always there when it comes to the first time introducing someone.

We booked dinner in a restaurant overlooking the Gardens where we first met in the UK. All of us arrived at the same time and had the most amazing night, Jay and Mom got along amazingly and he was such a gentleman, didn't let either of us do a thing, he opened doors, walked us home and for the first time ever... he stayed over at mine.

It was so important that Mom liked him, she is my world so that was huge for me! She made us tea and went to bed. Jay and I cuddled in on the sofa, I even introduced him to Monk and Luna, who also seemed to be Jays biggest fans! I was in a love bubble, this exact moment, I never wanted it to end. Everyone loved each other, we were safe, warm and as we shared kisses on the sofa, Jay just stopped, looked at me and once again at the exact same time it just felt right "I love you" we spoke softly. Once those words were spoken, we were smiling from ear to ear all night, got into bed and I fell asleep the happiest I've ever been.

Jay and I spoke every day, each visiting each other when we could. We spoke about adventures we wanted to do together and our motto was of course 'Crossing out the What Ifs'. We planned our next trip Interrailing around Italy, our first trip together, how exciting! We both worked our asses off saving for our future together, making amazing memories. Eventually it came the day we packed our suitcases, Jay stayed at mine that night as we had an early flight from Edinburgh the next day. We bounced out of bed that morning excited for what was to come. We headed to the airport, this time though we caught an Uber, I turned to do the familiar wave with mom on the way up the escalator and realised she wasn't there this time.

Was this the new chapter of my life, where I'm moving away from the comfort of my childhood home again? Surprisingly, I was overwhelmed with sadness. Jay spotted I was off and asked me what was wrong, I played it off for a bit until we got through security but he knew something wasn't right. "G, you can tell me, we talk about everything remember, you can always be authentically you, with me", he was right, I don't know why I was bottling up something so small, something I knew he could talk me through. I explained to him my thoughts and he understood, of course he did, we're the same person, remember?

He said my feelings are valid, it's another new journey filled with excitement, fear, upset and every type of emotion that comes with it.

We continued on through the terminal until we reached our gate. I loved having someone to do life with now, I still loved my solo trips and me time, but creating memories with someone you love is just so special! We boarded the plane, and don't forget we were still broke, so no, we didn't pay the extra £8 to sit beside each other! We went our separate ways to board the plane. I sat down pulled out my journal and began writing. After a quick flight, we landed in Zurich, I know we said Italy but this was one of the most amazing activities planned for this trip, we boarded the Bernina Express in Chur, a small town outside of Zurich, and began the journey through the snowy Alps and arrived into Tirano, another small village a short train ride from Milan. That train ride was on my bucket-list for years, I finally did it and it was so worth it!

We continued our travels from Milan to Venice to Verona to Rome, each more beautiful than the next! I fell in love with Italy, the food, the people, the architecture, it was just amazing. Having Jay there was amazing, I felt so safe, still felt at home with him and I trained him up to be an Instagram boyfriend so my feed was looking fire by the end of the trip!

He knew the journey I was on with myself and he was on his own journey, so he proposed we split up for a day in Rome. We explored by ourselves, I took myself out to lunch, enjoyed some amazing Pizza and Pasta, and visited the Trevi Fountain. With the exception of a few texts making sure we were both ok, the day we spent apart was great! I had to show off my new found confidence, practiced my Italian in a little restaurant and I wasn't afraid anymore.

We gathered together again back at the hotel, just in time for dinner. I went and freshened up for our meal at a gorgeous restaurant beside the Colosseum! Jay has always been such a gentleman so he'd give me my space when I'm getting ready and showering, but tonight I was just so I love, I called him in.

Jay slowly opened the door, asked if everything was ok. I knew if I didn't answer he'd come in. I was right, he opened the door and stepped in to see me perfectly ok, in the shower. I drew a love heart on the steamy glass and asked him if he wanted to join. I've never seen that man's face light up so quickly, I was curious to see if the gentleman had a bad side.

Let's just say.... he did.

The 10 minute shower went on a bit longer than usual, the floor was covered with suds and water but nothing mattered at that moment of time only us. We brought the passion from the shower to the bedroom, he covered me in kisses from my head to my toes, slowly lingering over the most intimate places. "Damn I didn't know he had this in him" I thought, "yeah we had sex before but this, this was next level, he took me places I didn't know I could get". He grabbed my hair, flipped me over and really took charge, of course being Jay, he checked in each time to make sure I was ok, but I was, I was more than ok!

When it was over, we laid there, trying to catch our breath. I listened to his heart beat through his chest and eventually we came back down to earth. "You are just amazing in every way possible G" he says still trying to catch his breath.

We get ready for the night, get changed and head to the restaurant. Walking hand in hand with Jay through the Roman Streets we come up to the amazing views of the Colosseum by night, all lit up and looking out of this world. We grabbed our seats and enjoyed the rest of the evening. Nothing could pop this love bubble we were in.

Eventually, the trip came to an end, returning home to Edinburgh. The goodbyes were extremely hard this time, even though he was only one hour away, we loved the time we spent together the last week and didn't want to leave each other.

"To love and to be loved is to feel the sun from both sides"

- David Viscott

Chapter 9 - New Beginnings

We had been together about 8 months now and everything was going great, so of course the conversations of getting our own place came up. We were both in jobs that we could change and relocate but who moves, is the big question. We didn't rush it, talked about it for a couple of weeks and decided Jay would move to Edinburgh which was amazing! It's funny how all of a sudden, I'm starting a life with someone I love, in a place I felt like I had to run away from all those years ago!

The day finally came after a lot of disappointment, missing out on our dream flat, lots of viewings, too much paperwork, but eventually we got a call from an agency.... It was ours, our dream flat in Edinburgh's West End, the top floor with amazing views of the park! Jay moved down the next week, we were so excited! I said my very temporary goodbyes to Mom, she only lived a 10 minute walk away now which was perfect!

We ordered the first takeaway for our first night in our own place, made a pillow fort and watched a movie. Then things took a turn I started feeling really sick, really bad cramps in my stomach and I knew something wasn't right. It didn't even enter our minds I could be pregnant, but we took a test, just to rule it out. We sat around the bathroom sink, in complete silence, those 3 minutes felt like an eternity...but then it appeared "Pregnant 3- weeks". Neither of us believed it, I burst out crying, Jay just held me but I could tell he was panicking. We just moved in together, were we ready for this?

I spent the next 2 days, cuddled up to Jay discussing the future, which all felt so up in the air at that moment. I booked in for a scan to double check and there it was, a real baby with a real heartbeat, that I was growing with the love of my life. The whole outlook on the pregnancy changed after that appointment. We were nervous but so excited to see what was to come.

The following weeks, we kept it a secret, I barely left the house because I spent the whole time getting sick thanks to 'morning sickness' which is a lie, they should call it 'morning, afternoon and night sickness' if you ask me! One evening, we were lying in bed and I felt a shooting pain I never felt before, Jay was asleep on my chest and he woke to me jolting with pain. We called the hospital and they advised me to come in.

The nurse did a scan, didn't say much, just left the room to fetch the doctor. A few minutes later, the doctor walks in with his head hanging low and delivers us the news no parent wants to hear. "I'm sorry..." that's

67

all I needed to hear, I bolted out of the hospital room, jumped into the car and bawled my eyes out. Jay grabbed some information leaflets for next steps and met me in the car. You could tell he was trying to hold it together for me, but he was upset too, he just lost a child too. All I wanted to do was curl up in bed and hug Mom, but she didn't even know, we were in the process of making the gift box to announce our pregnancy to her, now that's all over and I had no one to talk to! Yes, I had Jay, but we both needed our time to grieve alone.

A couple of days passed, I had miscarried naturally the day after the hospital so I didn't leave the house for about a week. I managed to pull myself out of bed and make something to eat after a while because Jay was getting worried. We had never seen each other like this, it was tough for both of us, we both needed to be held and told it was going to be ok so we gave each other some space when needed and eventually got through it together.

Nobody tells you the confusion and upset of losing a baby you didn't plan for in the first place.

A few of weeks passed and life was as normal as it could be, we were both back to work, trying to save for another adventure but the cost of rent and everything else wasn't exactly helping the situation. Eventually, we knew we needed a break after the heartbreak the last few months has brought, we dipped into our rainy-day fund and flew back to Ireland, the place I began to find a new me, start this journey of self and what eventually led me to Jason.

We booked the next flight to Cork and checked into the same hotel I stayed in previously. That's the best thing about Ireland, the people. The receptionist actually remembered me. She said she adored the Scottish accent so she could never forget me. "It's great to see you again Ms. Williams, you brought a handsome man on your travels this time, eh? I'm glad to see things are looking up for you, the beauty of Killarney I think" she winked at me, remembering how upset and lost I was last time I stayed here.

Jay & I made our way to the room. He spins me around, kisses my forehead, wraps his warm arms around me and says "I'm so proud of you G", this was out of nowhere but it was so needed. I really did change so much in the last 2 years since I left London. I'm stronger, more courageous, confident and in love with both myself and Jason! I am proud of me too!

 We spent the next few days exploring the town, visited the Waterfall, climbed Cardiac Hill, but this time I was able to turn around and say "do you see that?!" and someone was there sharing these memories with me. We sat at the top of the hill, devouring some amazing Tayto sandwiches of course, and just before we started the decent, Jay taps me on my shoulder, I turn around to find the man of my dreams, down on one knee with the most beautiful ring. I didn't even have to hear what he had to say it was immediately "YESSSS!". I was a fiancé, I had a fiancé, what is this life!?

We made our way down the hill, after I stopped crying and screaming with delight, and made it back to the hotel where he had arranged a whole dinner on the balcony, followed by some mocktails by the bar. The room was filled with rose petals and red balloons, I couldn't be happier!

The next day, we boarded our flight (as fiancées!!!!) and arrived home to tell Mom the news! She was so happy, I spent hours crying with happiness that day, it was perfect!

"New beginnings are the first steps towards transforming the impossible into the possible"

Chapter 10 - Panic

Life was going, nearly too perfect, if that's even possible. I had the man of my dreams, our dream flat, planning a wedding, just secured a job close to the house with my qualification and I had made amazing memories all while growing this amazing relationship with myself.

I panicked.

Is this my life now? Set in stone? I have everything I want, and I'm panicking!

I have so much more I want to do but I have rent to pay, a partner to factor into my decisions, a job I need to keep to provide for our future family.

I kept it to myself for a while weighing out my options to see what I really wanted and the questions just kept spinning in my head, over and over and over again. I knew it wouldn't stop until I got it out. I asked Jay for a chat, that evening we sat down and laid everything out on the table. Turns out, he too, felt the same way and was scared to tell me in case I felt unwanted or that he didn't appreciate what we had.

Jay wanted to visit Japan and a few more countries in Asia before properly settling down. I wanted to volunteer with children in Tanzania.

Two entirely different ideas, two big expenses that would be difficult to manage at the same time with rent due and all the other lovely adult expenses. But my motto, which turned into our motto is "Rule out the What Ifs" so, we discussed options and decided we aren't going to continue on with life wondering what if, about any experience and regretting it in years to come. We came to the conclusion; Jay will go on his trip to Tokyo while I stay here and hold the fort. Then once he returns, I will go to Tanzania and volunteer while Jay holds down the fort.

I loved how we could work together and both pushed each other to achieve our dreams.

The day came for Jay to leave, emotions were high, but we knew it wouldn't be for long and I couldn't want to hear all his stories once he returned. I spent the days, cleaning, meeting up with some of my friends from my Pilates classes, took a pottery class again, I remembered how much I loved that when I first moved home from London, it was just as fun and therapeutic too!

I may have popped into Ann Summers on my walk to 'fill the gap' from Jay being away. I spent time with Mom, had a girl's night and a sleepover which was so nice to have that time together. I feel in all the hustle and bustle of work and adulting, it's hard to find the time to be with the people you love most.

The weeks flew by and Jay returned, I haven't seen him this happy in a long time. I loved seeing him light up, telling all his stories from the travels, trying the Japanese snacks he brought back and feel like I was there with him through his amazing pictures.

Two weeks later, it was my turn, Jay dropped me to the airport. I turned to him to wave goodbye and my heart broke, but I knew what I was doing was right. I still need me time and I have to enjoy the time I'm able to pack up and go like this. I couldn't wait to tell him all my stories once I returned.

I boarded the plane, turned on the good ol' reliable Hannah Montana movie and slept for most of the flight. I touched down in Tanzania at nearly midnight, so I made my way to the group accommodation and settled in for the night.

Once morning came, we were all called to the kitchen
to introduce ourselves. This reminded me of my trip to
Thailand where I met my now fiancé. I look to my left
and who had appeared? Megan, from the Thailand trip,
I couldn't believe it!

She had spent the last 2.5 years travelling and said that
I had inspired her to keep going and continue to rule
out the what ifs! She explained how it's tough having no
base, nowhere to really call home and no partner but
she said all the memories she has made have been
worth it! This is her last trip before finally heading back
to Ireland and seeing her family again. Her grandmother
had passed away in the meantime but she was in
Australia at the time and just couldn't afford to pay for
the flight home. She said it was one of the toughest
decisions she had to make, she felt horrible and selfish
but the decision was made, there was no going back
now. Her eyes began to fill with tears "that's why I
came to Tanzania" she said, "it was my grandmothers
dream, she loved helping people and regretted not
taking the time from her life and flying out here to
help. I couldn't make it back for the funeral for her so I
said I could at least make her dream come true, through
me". It was amazing so see such strength but it also hit
me with such mixed emotions, the joy that I made the
decision to come here even when everything back home
was going perfectly and that I won't pass away
wondering what if. But I also realised, Mom has grown
3 years older too, does she have any regrets, any dreams
she wants to achieve?

Megan and I continued to talk the whole day, I told her how I'm now engaged to Jason, she couldn't believe it! And how we're living in Edinburgh full time. I was happy speaking about my life, I was so proud of what I had achieved in the last few years. All of these achievements, all because of one decision made in the midst of misery and feeling lost in London.

The next day we began volunteering with the school children, we played, taught English, showed them some pictures from home and just made the best little friends ever. It was so inspiring to see how happy these children were even without materialistic things we all take for granted! They played outside with a football made from various materials, drew hopscotch on the ground with a stone and sang together in gratitude for the food they got to share together. This trip had changed my outlook on life, big time.

After 2 weeks of amazing adventures through a safari, playing with the children, trying the local food, experiencing different cultures, it was time to go home. Megan and I swapped numbers and decided to meet once she returned home.

I realised, I had so much fun, learned so much and loved so dearly, by myself. I understood now that happiness was learning to live with myself, my happiness was never in anyone else's hands and true happiness comes from within. If you experience it with anyone else, that's just a bonus!

I boarded the flight home, buzzing with excitement to see Jay and Mom again! To my surprise both of them were there at the arrivals gate, running to hug me! "I love my life" I thought to myself, "I love my people too!"

The car ride home was a short one, but I packed as many stories into it as I could. As if I wasn't going to talk Jays ear off all night about it and repeat myself all over again to Mom tomorrow!

"Panicking is a reaction, not a plan"

– Liane Moriarty

Chapter 11 - Settling Down

Was this it? We've both ticked off our bucket lists, both have a job we enjoy, we're planning a wedding and have talked about our future together. Are we really ready to settle down?

People say "Once you have kids your life is over" "As soon as you take out that mortgage, wave fancy holidays goodbye" but I don't think that's the case, neither does Jay. We can't wait to start a family together and make more memories with our children.

But.

Are we really ready? This circled my mind every day for months after the Tanzania trip. After the miscarriage last year, I was scared to try for a baby, I couldn't deal with that loss again. My due date came around, Jay and I, went to Portobello beach, laid out a picnic blanket and just took the day for us, we did whatever we wanted to do, we cried, imagined what they'd look like, smiled thinking of decorating the nursery together and most importantly just held each other.

We decided to take the first step and apply for a mortgage, after months of rejections and lots of paperwork, it was finally approved! We knew our budget and began the house hunt. It's tough out there, we viewed over 100 houses, applied for a handful getting denied from each one. Until one day, our dream house in North Berwick appeared, it was just outside Edinburgh City, overlooking the sea. It had a huge master bedroom as well as two smaller rooms which we would hopefully convert into rooms for our children sometime in the future.

We weren't the most religious people but my god did we pray for that house! It was going to be ours I just knew it, and with that, 3 weeks later, we were signing the papers and getting the keys.

This was it, our dream house, we bought it together, it was in the most beautiful location and so close to Mom as well!

We moved our stuff from our small flat, into what felt like a mansion, unloaded all of our boxes, hung pictures of us on the walls and added all of our magnets we collected from our travels, to the fridge.

We have never been happier; things were coming together for us both and we had nothing but hope for the future.

That was until, Mom called, "it's Luna" she said, my
now 14-year-old 'puppy' I've had since a teenager, wasn't
doing too well. That dog has been through everything
with me, the highs, the lows. She watched me pass
through the house in each chapter of my life, she
cuddled into me and kept me company when I moved
back from London, she was my world. That's the thing
about growing up, your childhood dog doesn't have the
same lifespan as you do, it's the worst thing you've to
face, but it is inevitable. I dropped the boxes and drove
to Moms. I swung open the door to see Mom sat on the
ground rubbing Lunas head as she looked so
comfortable in her fluffy new bed Mom had just got
her.

I cuddled up beside her, held her paw and lay my head
on her tummy. She looked at me, gave me one last wag
of her tail and slipped away. It's like she was waiting for
me to say goodbye before she left. She was my baby;
Moms best friend and she kept Mom company when I
was away living my own life.

I stayed with Mom that night, we cuddled up on the
sofa, looking and pictures from when she was a puppy
up until now. We laughed and cried but we knew she
had a great life, a long life and it was her time to go, we
were just glad it was peaceful.

The next morning, Mom decided to meet up with some friends to take her mind off things. I went back to the house to continue unpacking, it's strange when a pet dies, because it's not classed as this major loss, you're expected to carry on with your life straight away, when in reality, they are a part of your family for nearly 15 years, they are family.

Jay held me while I cried that day, he did most of the unpacking.

The following days after Lunas passing, life carried on as normal, the excitement was back about this new chapter and there was one more surprise....

Jay walked into the kitchen with his hands wrapped around my eyes as a blindfold. I peeled back his hands, to be met by Lily, a gorgeous black and white springer spaniel covered in freckles. I fell in love instantly; we had our own little family in our new family home! Jay was terrified it was too soon after Lunas passing but it was just what I needed.

"Settling Down is not the end of adventure; it is the beginning of the greatest one"

Chapter 12 - Roommate Phase

Oooo, the dreaded roommate phase. I think every couple experiences this as some point or another. I loved Jay to bits and I knew he loved me, but the love bubble was burst. We were together over 3 years now, the stress of the move took over, the wedding planning was driving us both crazy and as it says on the tin - we were officially entering the roommate phase.

We woke up, made breakfast at separate times, there was no coffee in bed in the mornings, no more talk of children, came back from work, ate dinner, watched TV in silence at opposite ends of the sofa, argued about who had to walk the dog, and went asleep to repeat it all the next day.

Everyone may have seen us as the perfect couple, great communication, loved up, building a future together, trusted each other 100% but that doesn't last forever I suppose! Our communication was in the form of an argument, "love you" was just a habit to say before turning the opposite way in bed, sex was like a chore and everything just felt shit.

This went on for a couple of months before we both said, we have a wedding coming up, we either try to fix this or call it now. We both knew this wasn't the end, we just needed the spark back.

We went to couples counselling once, which we both hated. So, we decided to do it ourselves! We made time for each other each evening, we'd walk Lily together and have chats along the way like we used to! Slowly but surely the coffee in bed was a regular thing again, we cooked dinner together, we baked together, had our alone time with our friends but also made time for each other.

The journey we went on individually these last couple of years, single handedly saved our relationship, I think. We were both strong individuals, who loved ourselves first, realised what we cared about and fought for it.

Since then, it's never been better, we laugh again, we dance around like weirdos in the living room, we have steamy hot sex again and we cannot wait for this wedding!!

With only 2 months until the wedding, we put the finishing touches on all of our plans. We both wanted a small wedding in Italy, the place we fell even more in love with each other on our first trip together all those years ago. We had booked the most amazing villa, seating 20 people and a spectacular backdrop overlooking Lake Como. Lily was our Ring Bearer, Megan was my maid of hour, and Julie, Jays sister was my bridesmaid. Jay had his boys supporting him too!

"Love is a fire. But whether it is going to warm your heart or burn your house down, you can never tell"

– Joan Crawford

Chapter 13 - Family time

Family.... It can be a touchy word, but I heard something a while back that I love "You get two families, the one you're born into and the one you create". I love that thought! Dad wasn't really in my life that much so it was always just me and Mom, which was great, don't get me wrong! But I always said I'm going to make sure I choose not only a life partner for me but a great dad to my children.

I genuinely think I have found that in Jay, he is so caring, loving, mature and so god damn sexy- ooops, you can tell it's ovulation time and we have been trying for a baby these last few weeks!

That is one thing I love about the whole baby making process, it's like a reward up front for all the sickness, mood swings, broken sleep and body aches you are about to endure once you're pregnant!

The sex though, it was amazing! I don't know what has come over us, we're trying positions we've never even heard of, it's a side to each other we've never seen before! Between the sexy messages all day long about what's gonna happen when he's home, the raunchy pictures from the shower, the sex on every surface we can find. It has been mind blowing!

In light of trying new things, I popped into Ann Summers, bought a couples game of Karma Sutra, and we played it all weekend! I genuinely don't think we left the house from Friday night to Monday morning. Things got messy, there was everything from whipped cream to whips and god was I loving it! My favourite has to be the new toy we got, Jay lies me on the bed, ties each hand to a corner of the bed, teases me the whole way down to my toes, ties my ankles to the bottom corners of the bed so I cannot move. This is then followed by our new bottle of chocolate body paint being dripped all over my body, while he uses his tongue to lick up every, last, drop. This drives me wild, I want to squirm and grab his hair but I physically cannot move. It's so interesting seeing this side of Jay. He goes from opening doors and bringing me coffee, to tying me up, getting off on the fact I'm helpless. I have to say, I am not complaining! I like a man who can do it all!

A few weeks passed, it was 2 days to go until the wedding, we were sat in our Villa in Italy, this was the final chance to see if all that baby making paid off, we took a pregnancy test, this time instead of being nervous, waiting a lifetime for time to pass, we turned on High School Musicals playlist and danced until the 3 minutes were over.... We turned the test over but neither of us could look, we decided to countdown "3....2....1....Aghhhhhhhhh!!!!" We were pregnant! Those 2 lines were so strong! I couldn't believe it, I started crying and so did Jay, but this time it was with complete and utter happiness! "Our baby is going to be here for our wedding day" I whispered. "Our first baby is going to be here too, looking over us G" said Jay, of course that set me off crying again but it was such a beautiful moment I didn't want it to end.

We parted ways, holding onto our little secret for a bit longer. It was time for our rehearsal dinner. I had picked a floor length cream dress with lace frills on the neckline, Jay looked handsome as ever in his suit pants and fitted shirt! The dinner went amazing, it was so lovely being able to have everyone we loved in one room, Mom and Jays mom were there, Megan travelled over with her new boyfriend (they are so cute I love them together!!), Lily joined the party running around like a headless chicken as per usual, typical Springer Spaniel I suppose! We were joined by a few friends from home and a couple of work colleagues and that's it! I couldn't have asked for anything more!

The day was here, Mom, Megan and Jays sister, Julie, all helped me get ready, hair and makeup was done, dresses were on and we were ready to go!

I had a few minutes alone with Mom, "another chapter of my life unfolds I suppose" I shrugged, holding back the tears. "I wouldn't be here if it wasn't for you Mom, you made sure I saw my potential, pushed me to take risks and by taking that risk I met my soon to be Husband, I couldn't be more grateful to you". We hugged for a bit, had a dance to some Abba and then I decided it was time...

"If I'm half the mother you are, I'll be a damn good one, I guess we'll find out soon though, isn't that right Nan?" I pulled the test from my bag, Mom burst out in tears of joy! I was so happy to be able to share these moments with her before I change my name for good.

"You get two families, the one you're born into and the one you choose"

Chapter 14 - A New Identity

I found myself in a new situation, I'm no longer Miss Williams, I am Mrs. Rogers. I'm no longer a girlfriend, I'm a wife. I'm no longer a tenant, I'm a homeowner. I am no longer just a daughter, I am a Mom.

All these changes in the space of less than a year. It's nearly a whole new identity to adjust to so quickly!

People don't realise how much it plays with your brain when your identity changes like that. I used to be just Georgia, a party girl who still smashed it in school. Now I have responsibilities, adult titles and a whole new world to live in!

I let this thought sit with me for a while, there were a lot of emotions coming up that were valid in the situation. I was confused, worried, excited, happy but I was also grieving. I was grieving the old me, Georgia Williams, hopeless at dating yet crazy confident, scared to break the 'norm' but the girl who did it anyway, the child in me that wasn't afraid to dance like nobody was watching. There was a lot to miss in Georgia Williams, but that girl led me to where I was now. At the beginning of my story, I said "if you asked me my qualities I would say lost, uninspired, lazy, lonely, single, introvert with crippling social anxiety". I was right when I said this is a broad question with ever changing answers, because right now my qualities are "Loyal, Courageous, Loved, Calm and Inspired by all the amazing people I surround myself with". I may have said I wanted it all by 25, but here I am, I have it all now, it may be 4 years later but there's no set timeline, what's meant for you won't pass you and the universe will time it right, let go of the reigns and the rest will fall into place.

I was so excited for this new chapter, Jay had started his own business after years of hard work, I was quietly expanding my portfolio to take up writing full time. Things were falling into place just right.

Our first ultrasound appointment came around just before the honeymoon, the nerves went through the roof as we stepped foot into the hospital, the last time we were here we lost our baby so that was always lingering over us. Jay held my hand as we walked down the never-ending corridor, the closer we got, the sweatier our palms were. "We got this G" he whispered, trying to reassure me when I could feel his grip tightening with fear. We sat in the waiting room, looking at all the women with their full term bumps, some in the same position we were, over 3 years ago now.

"Mrs. Rodgers" they called from behind the reception desk, to which I didn't react. Jay nudged me, "that's you, wife" he said, I was so anxious I completely forgot the new me!

I stood up grabbed Jays hand and walked into the room. The nurse invited me to sit on the bed. "Is this your first?" she says, to which I just lowered my head. Jay put his hand on my leg and says "second, we miscarried a couple of years ago, so this baby was handpicked by their own sibling, there's something special about that" gosh he always knows what to say, I looked at him and smiled. The nurse proceeded to add the gel and look for a heartbeat, each second feeling like a lifetime. There it was, their heartbeat, the perfect little bean on the screen. The room immediately felt more relaxed, the next time we would be there we would find out if it was a boy or girl. I had a gut feeling it was a little girl, Jay was thinking a boy. Either way, all we wanted was a healthy baby.

We returned home, collected our suitcases, dropped Lily to my Moms house and off we went on our honeymoon. Next stop, France!

We had treated ourselves to our first ever 5 star hotel, in the centre of Paris overlooking the Eiffel Tower. We landed into Charles De Gaulle Airport, jumped in a taxi, arrived to the hotel and were greeted by chocolates, rose petals and a candlelit entrance to the room.

We stood on the balcony and just held each other while we watched the world go by below.

"A girl should be two things; who and what she wants"

- Coco Chanel

Chapter 15 - Passion

I slipped into something a bit more comfortable, I knew Jay loved red, and it's a colour I felt most confident in, I came out of the bathroom in my red, lace one piece lingerie covered with a robe. Jay was preoccupied ordering us drinks to the balcony (non-alcoholic of course!), he turned around, I dropped my robe and called him over to the bed. He made his way over to me, handcuffed my arms to the bed frame and teased me with my own toy, I was dying for him, I craved him and his manliness and he knew it. Just as he started, there was a knock on the door.

Our drinks had arrived, he put them on ice, picked an ice cube out of the bucket and decided this was his next move. He teased me for what felt like forever. He had the ice cube between his lips and ran it over every inch of my body, the ice cube melted and he continued to work wonders, pulling away each time I got close. He catered for all of my needs that night and knew exactly how to drive me wild! All of a sudden, I was blindfolded and brought to the balcony, we were on the 12th floor so the wind on my skin made me feel every touch, more intense. I felt the handcuffs attach to the metal barrier on the balcony. He ran his hands down my chest, along my stomach and stopped right at my thighs. "What's your name" he whispered in my ear, "Mrs. Rogers" I grinned back, knowing how he loved that I have his name now, I was his and he was mine.

He took off the blindfold, I was completely exposed, with only his hands as a bra, the Eiffel Tower sparkled as he bent me over the table and gave me the best sex of my life!

I loved this side to us, the sexual chemistry was never fading, we had so much love for each other and we would protect one another, no matter what.

This holiday was about us, probably our last holiday as 2, we were determined to make it special. The next morning, we ordered breakfast in bed. It was perfect, just my husband and I, wearing nothing but the bed sheets, eating croissants, looking out over the Eiffel Tower.

We finally got dressed, headed downstairs and went exploring all Paris had to offer. We took all the typical tourist photos, caught the metro with no destination in mind, we were just happy spending this time together, back in our love bubble.

To my surprise Jay had booked a date for us that night, we arrived back to the hotel, Jay had arranged a dress for me to wear and just led the way. I saw the boat from the distance but couldn't believe it was for me. A candlelit boat, along the Seine, with a traditional French musician accompanying us on the trip. I felt like an imposter, how is this my life? I don't deserve this, I thought to myself. But once again, in that exact moment, Jay whispered in my ear "You deserve this G, you are superwoman, growing our child, building a business, supporting me in every decision, and most importantly you chose you, you prioritised falling in love with yourself first before letting me in and I think that is what has allowed us to have this beautiful life together. I didn't want a holiday romance, I saw what we had straight away but I also saw how strong and confident you were with your decisions and knew it was the right thing plus I knew we'd find our way back together, look at us now!". I cuddled into his chest, and it felt like that night was a dream.

"Sex is more than an act of pleasure; it is the ability to be able to feel so close to a person, so connected, so comfortable that it's almost breathtaking to the point you feel you can't take it. And at this moment you're a part of them" - Thom Yorke

Chapter 16 - The Bump

We returned from Paris, all loved up and truly in that 'Honeymoon' Phase everyone talks about.

First stop was Moms house, said hello, told her the amazing stories from Paris and collected Lily! We arrived back to our house, feeling like this was really the beginning of our favourite chapter.

Lily walked in ahead of us (checking the house for burglars I assume, just as well there wasn't any because she'd just piss all over the floor and hide behind us, we pretend she's a great guard dog though!)

We added our newest magnet to the fridge, this was our thing, each country we visited, a magnet was added, a cute reminder of the amazing memories we made together!

Just as I sat down, I got a call from the hospital, "Good Afternoon, Mrs. Rogers, just checking you're still ok for your appointment at 1pm?". I looked at the clock, it read 1:05pm. "I'm so sorry, we're just stuck in traffic, we should be there in 10!" I lied of course, but she didn't know that. How could we forget the gender reveal day!

I hated being late, I think it was ingrained into me with my social anxiety, I never wanted to be the last person to walk into a big crowd! We jumped in the car and raced to the hospital. I think once we arrived the nurse knew we forgot. I was wearing a bodysuit, who wears a bodysuit to a scan?! That just means getting your - "omg frilly, red bra, really Georgia!?" I thought to myself as I pulled down the straps of the suit, I was mortified! I looked at Jay and he was red in the face trying to hold back the laughter, when he laughs, I laugh and I couldn't contain it so I just burst out laughing in the nurse's face! "I'm so sorry, we just got back from our Honeymoon and completely forgot about the appointment - hence the *cough* outfit choice". Thankfully the nurse laughed with us (possibly at us, but let's think optimistically, eh?). She added the gel once again, wiggled around the probe and I grabbed Jays hand, bracing myself for the news. "Wait!" I said, "Can you just put it in an envelope and we can open it ourselves later?", the nurse agreed while Jay looked very confused.

I realised I never planned the gender reveal because I wasn't sure I'd make it to this point in my pregnancy after what happened to my last one. I didn't want to get my hopes up. But this time was different, I wanted it to be special, more intimate than a hospital room. We got the results, slipped the envelope into Jays pocket and made our way to the car.

On the drive home, we pulled into Sainsburys, I passed the envelope to a shop worker and said please pick out 1 outfit and 2 cupcakes the colour of the gender. The girl was probably only 16, and probably thought I was crazy! I didn't care though. This was my special moment and I was so excited! It may not have been these big extravagant reveals you see on Instagram with fireworks and smoke but it was special to us!

I secured the goods, went to the car and we parked up at Portobello beach. It was sunset by the time we collected Lily from the house and got back out to the beach. We had to include her, she joined this little family of ours and wanted her to be a part of this occasion too! We knew our Angel Baby was looking down on us too, as the last beam of sun shone down on the bag. I cried for a little, we held each other and eventually pulled the cupcakes from the bag. We took one big bite with our eyes closed and pulled the outfit out of the bag and laid it in the sand. "1...2...3...it's a girl!!!!" Our very own baby girl, I couldn't believe it! Jay wrapped his arms around me and said "I can't wait to meet her, if she's anything like her mom, she's going to be strong and beautiful!". We just sat on the sand for a while, taking in the moment. I'm so glad we stopped the nurse last second and had this moment to ourselves, it was perfect!

Officially in my 2nd trimester, I was starting to show. People were slowly finding out! Jay was obsessed with my bump, he tried hyping me up but I just felt horrible, the morning sickness kicked in, I felt bloated and horrible. Nothing fit me anymore and I hated how my body looked.

I was at the stage where, I looked pregnant, but didn't look pregnant if that makes sense. I resorted to big jumpers and leggings to hide my growing belly. This was hard for me because I spent so much time, working on me, feeling the best I've felt in a long time, ensuring I put effort into my everyday look so I felt good in my own body.

I know I should be grateful for a healthy pregnancy, and I was, but these are some of the things that were tough. I knew the end result would be worth it though!

The weekend came around, Jay was off weekends so we got to spend some well needed time together. He was late coming home from work that Friday evening, which was strange for him. He walked in the door an hour later than usual, but with 2 bags in his hands. He opened one bag, filled with all my favourite sweets. The other, contained a beautiful red, floor length dress. I immediately started crying, the hormones took over of course, but how did I get so lucky with him? I felt like a horrible wife, lazing around the house, looking like Adam Sandler and the sex was non-existent anymore. "Let's go G, get ready, I'm taking you somewhere special" he said.

I walked to the bedroom, took off the oversized, BO smelling clothes I had been in for days and jumped in the shower. Jay knocks on the bathroom door and comes in. "Do you need a hand?" He laughed, while stripping off and stepping into the shower with me. He massaged the shampoo into my scalp, rinsed it out, used my loofah all over my body and kissed my neck, so gently. There was something so special about this, there was no expectations for sex, it was just love and care of the highest degree. We left the shower, back to the bedroom. He held open my new dress as I stood one foot in at a time, he placed the straps over my arms and under his breath he said "shit".

My mind raced, "oh no all this effort and it doesn't even fit, or it looks shit - I knew it" I thought to myself. "You look amazing G, I think it just makes it hotter that you're growing our child in there!" he reassured me with a gentle slap on my bum!

I did my hair and makeup, said goodnight to Lily and left the house with no idea where I was going. We drove into the city, pulled up outside The Dome, the most magnificent restaurant in Edinburgh (imo!). We walked through the revolving doors, into the main hall. The main hall was out of this world, a bar in the middle overlooked by a giant chandelier, thousands of paintings and a pianist in the corner. The staff greeted us, took us to our table and gave us the menus. I couldn't believe he had done this for me, he just finished a week of work and his priority was taking me out to dinner? God, I love him! We held hands across the table, enjoyed the amazing food and spoke about everything, all night.

This was so needed. I didn't recognise the Georgia that was sitting at home.

We got home that night, that dress came off as quick as lightening, I threw on a pair of Jays boxers and jumped into bed. I pulled a makeup wipe from my bedside locker, half asleep, I smeared it all over my face before apparently falling asleep with the wipe lying over my face and the makeup still intact. Jay came into bed and cleaned me up thankfully!

"A baby bump is the sweetest sight to behold, a promise of new life and endless love"

Chapter 17 - The Memory Box

While I was trying to preoccupy myself by cleaning, I pulled out a couple of boxes under the bed that I had completely forgotten about!

I opened box number one, my baby box, Mom had gathered all my things since the moment she knew she was having me and put them all in this box to give to me on my 21st birthday, a tradition I hope to carry on with my kids.

I looked through it, pulling out her pregnancy test, the screen just showing yellow now, inside of the bright 2 lines.

My first shoes, little red booties, I could probably still pull these off if I could get some in my size (I was a stylish baby it seems!).

My first curl, bright platinum blonde hair, you wouldn't think it looking at me now with Dark Brown hair, but I do still call myself a natural blonde, in complete denial it darkened over the years.

Mom tied our hospital bands together for keepsake too, "Baby Williams" it read alongside my date and time of birth.

The rest of the box was filled with school report cards, birthday cards from loved ones (some of which have now passed away so these were lovely to have), medals from my sports days and even my first Valentines card, that I'm still convinced Mom wrote for me!

I sat with this box, looking at the journey of my life, thinking about how Mom was once in my position, excited for what was to come. It brought a lot of memories up, some good, some bad...the day Dad left, my first boyfriend, my school graduation. It was nice to look back and remember all the moments that made me, me.

Box 2 was labelled "Us", I secretly collected all of the memories Jay and I made together, throughout the years. Everything from the first train ticket to Glasgow, a picture of us at the Phi Phi Islands, the receipt from the first meal we ate together in Edinburgh when we arrived back from Bali to our Marriage Certificate. We had come such a long way, there was ups and downs but we created a life together. Life is full of speed bumps but we made it through them all, the loss of our first baby, the wedding, the roommate phase, buying our own house and now we were awaiting the arrival of our rainbow baby. I couldn't have asked for a better person to do life with.

Jay walked into the room; he never saw any of this before. We sat on the floor, looking through all of our amazing memories. We did it, we lived by "Ruling out the What Ifs". We were able to look back and have no regrets. Jay lifted our angel baby's pregnancy test from the box, "it's really still showing positive?" He looks at me in disbelief. "Baby bean was real Jay, they're always with us" I said cuddling into him. We spent the next half an hour laughing and reminiscing on our memories. Jay stood up, went to his bedside locker and pulled out a plastic bag. "It may be a lot less aesthetic than yours but I saved everything too, G". To my surprise he had everything, his first train ticket to Edinburgh, our first texts printed off, a note with all my favourite things so he wouldn't forget at the beginning, a dried flower from the first bouquet he got me and a gift receipt for my engagement ring. I looked at the receipt, it read "July 2020", "Jay.. this was the date you first arrived to Edinburgh!" He laughed as his face went bright red. "On my way back to the train after our first kiss, I knew you were the one, I couldn't imagine life with anyone else", I burst out crying, "Why did you wait so long you prick!" I said laughing.

"I was letting you cross out the what ifs G, until the day I decided to put that motto to use. I carried the ring with me everywhere, when we climbed cardiac hill in Ireland, I sat at the top watching the joy on your face and thought, what if I miss my chance with her, what if she says yes and we live happily ever after? So that's when I decided to make you mine forever".

111

I knew Jay was romantic but I wasn't expecting that! We really were living our happy ever after!

Jay saw a slip of paper hanging out from the side of my baby box. "30 before 30" he said smiling. I completely forgot about that! When mom gave me the box on my 21st, I had to write a 30 before 30 list and work my way through it for the next 9 years. "Well, I've 6 months to do whatever is on that list" I laughed.

It read:

1.   Get married to the love of my life
2.   Travel to the Phi Phi Islands
3.   Stop caring what everyone thinks
4.   Ride the Bernina Express
5.   Skydive
6.   Go on a cruise
7.   Get up and sing at a Karaoke Night
8.   Travel Italy
9.   See the Eiffel Tower
10. Buy a house
11. Get pregnant
12. Get your own dog
13. Visit Ireland
14. Climb a mountain
15. Volunteer in a 3rd world country
16. Drink out of a chocolate fountain

17. Film a private sex tape
18. Give up alcohol
19. Learn to drive
20. Swim with Dolphins
21. Visit Bali
22. Don't get old and gross
23. Stay blonde!
24. Get a tattoo
25. Buy mom a holiday
26. Start Pilates
27. Be me
28. Be happy
29. Write a book.
30. Make it to 30.

As Jay read them out, I was ticking the ones I've done off the list! 19 down, 11 to go! Jay sniggered while pointing at numbers 7,9 and 17. "I think you 'nailed' number 9 anyway" he laughed, thinking back on that amazing night on the balcony in Paris.

"I'm very curious to see number 7, and I would happily aid you in ticking off number 17" he grinned.

I looked at the list, "I'm never gonna get through all this, I'm also 4 months pregnant may I add!"

21 year old me and 29 year old me were different people with different ideas! I hated being blonde and

dyed it brown when I was 24 so that's crossed off the list, sorry younger Georgia!

"You can cross number 22 off the list too!" Jay adds. "You are far from old and gross; you're a sexy momma and you don't look a day older than the day I met you!" I scoffed while he crossed that out too.

Ok, 9 to go, that's not too bad! Chocolate fountain idea fits in perfectly with my pregnancy cravings too!

A couple days went by and I forgot about the list, thanks to baby brain! Jay didn't though, he marched through the door that day, with a large box under his arm. I was sceptical but who doesn't love a good parcel coming through the door!?

He was like a child at show and tell, held the box behind his back, grinning from ear to ear. "Sooo... about that list, I got all that you need". I was already nervous, what in gods name has he bought?

First, he pulled out a chocolate fountain, my very own chocolate fountain, in my house?! I couldn't complain about that! Next came a bag of rose petals, a new toy from Ann Summers and a tripod, now this turned my stomach, I'm not sure if it was a good reaction or a bad one but I was weary for what's to come next. "Drumroll pleaseeeee......" he shouts, lifting the last thing from the box, a Karaoke Machine, oh lord. "Because we don't do bars and I know you're not feeling your best lately, we're bringing the Karaoke night to our living room, get practicing!!". What have I done? I really can't be fucked with this now, I feel like shit. Jay went to so much effort and was so excited though so I put on a brave face for the evening.

The only thing that was used out of that box for the next week was the chocolate fountain, I happily ticked that off my list! 8 to go...

The bad mood passed and I was feeling a bit more like myself again so I took this rare moment and did as much as I could! Karaoke Night it was!

Jay set up the living room with disco lights, a table in the middle with 2 ice cold mocktails for us to enjoy. "Sing King Karaoke" appeared on the TV, reminding me of the days Mom left me at home by myself for the first few times and I slaughtered every song that came on.

I drank my homemade mocktail, stood up and called Jay on stage for a duet. Neither of us had a note between us but that didn't matter, it was me and him, enjoying time together and singing our hearts out to "Start of Something New from High School Musical". We sang and laughed for hours before we were too tired to do anymore!

I grabbed a spoon, had one more slurp from the chocolate fountain and went to bed.

The next weekend came around, Jay had once again come home with a bag under his arm. If you hadn't guessed, his love languages were words of affirmation and acts of service. This time, he pulled out a red fishnet jumpsuit, "you still have those red heels from Paris?" he asked with a grin on his face. I think he forgot I was now 5 months pregnant. I was fully sure my bump would burst the netting! But I was in the mood for some fun, to feel sexy again and just some time with him.

I grabbed the new outfit, squeezed into my heels and with all the netting still intact, I walked my way into Jay, who was eagerly awaiting the results of his purchase. I followed the rose petals to the room, saw a silk bedsheet and the camera perched in the corner on the new tripod. I tried my best to play it off, trying a bit too hard to ignore the camera filming us. Jay saw I was uncomfortable and asked if I wanted to stop or turn off the camera. He also explained how no one was watching, it was me and him, together, having a bit of fun making memories to look back on!

He was right, I had worked myself up so much, you would've thought it was being broadcasted live to national television. We did our thing and god it was good, the bump forced us into some new positions, but they were amazing. There was something so hot about the camera watching us all of a sudden, the feelings took over and I was so into it now, I was tied to the bedposts getting cream licked off me like a dessert. We finished the 'movie' and sat back laughing at what just happened. Another thing ticked off the list I suppose! "Thank you 21 year old Georgia for adding that to the list!" I laughed! "7 to go!!"

Next up was buying Mom a holiday, she has helped us so much with prepping for baby girl to arrive and I've always wanted to be in the position to pay for her to have a break. We drove to her house, had a cup of tea and chatted for a while before I said "What're you up to this weekend?" her usual reply of "oh you know, the usual, go for a walk, do the shopping and see the girls at Bingo on Sunday I suppose!". I loved she still had her routine, still met the girls and had the chats. "Nope!" I said, "pack your bags because you leave for Ireland on Friday morning!", she looked at me in disbelief.

I know it wasn't much but Mom didn't like sun holidays and she wasn't the most confident at travelling by herself so I sent her where I knew she'd be looked after, Killarney!

"What, why, what do you mean, you're fibbing Georgia!" She stuttered. I handed her the boarding pass and let her know the plans.

"I was talking to Megan, she will meet you at Cork Airport and drive you to Killarney. You'll stay at the hotel I've stayed at before, they're so lovely there so make sure you ask for what you need ok?" I tried to reassure her. She seemed nervous but excited, just like I felt the day I went there for the first time.

It felt amazing to be able to do this for her, I couldn't wait to hear her stories!

Let's see... skydive, cruise, tattoo... a few more remained, with only 4 months left until my birthday and just over 4 months left until baby is here too. I think the skydive was very unlikely cause you know, it's kind of illegal to skydive with a baby inside you! But tattoo time, I suppose!

Jay already had a few tattoos, that's another feature I loved on him, tattoos marking out his milestones, all over his big muscles. He agreed to get one with me for support, he already had one booked in for baby girl so there was no need for him to book another one but here we were! I had chosen a small "J" to go on my ring finger, directly under my ring, so then whenever I

118

couldn't wear my ring, I still had something! Jay did the same, "G" was initialled onto his ring finger - of course he didn't seem phased in the slightest - while I sat watching, with sweat pumping out of every pore in my body. Only then while anxiously reading the signs on the wall, I spotted "Unable to tattoo anyone: Under 18, Intoxicated, Pregnant...." How could I not have thought of that! I was so annoyed at myself but secretly happy I didn't have to go through with it! "oh shit, well it's paid for now so I suppose we can reschedule for after baby's here? I'll be coming in anyway so you can join me, agreed?" Says Jay grinning away as per usual. I agree, we postpone for now, Jay looks at me as we walk out of the tattoo parlour "you really think you can get away with it that easy?", I laugh and reply "It's booked before 30 so I guess that counts!"

As soon as that left my mouth, I knew I dug myself a hole "hmmm I suppose you could do the same with the skydive babe? I know you hate not ticking off everything on a list", Jay knew exactly what he was doing, I hated and loved him for it! 30 minutes passed and apparently, I was booked in to throw myself 10,000ft out of a plane, with a baby (who at the time of the jump would be 6months old) that I need to get back home alive for!

In the meantime, Mom had returned from her trip to Ireland. We called over to hear all her stories. I haven't seen her this happy in a long time! She told us all about

119

her stay, visiting the waterfall and she even climbed up Cardiac Hill where me and Jay got engaged! After lots of storytelling, blurry pictures and 'mom' selfies, she wrapped her arms around me and thanked me for the experience! At the very end, she decided to tell us the most important part. She too, met someone! An Irish guy, born and raised in Killarney. If you've ever been, you would remember the horse and carts that did tours around the town. Mom had decided to take a tour and rest her legs, the horse walked through the national park, past the castle and along the lake. During that time, she was chatting to the 'jarvey', he is the guy that steers the horse and cart. They were the same age, both had one daughter each and Mom explained how they were in similar stages in life, not knowing what to do while everyone they cared about moved on with their lives. Long story short, they hit it off! They exchanged numbers and he was coming to visit Edinburgh next weekend to see her! I was so happy for her; she deserved all this! Since Dad left, she spent her time raising me and always being there for me. Sure, she has her friends but I always wanted her to find someone to spend the rest of her life with, and this may be him! She skipped into the kitchen with this new lease of life and said she must go and get her hair done before he arrives! We left her to it, gave her a hug and said our goodbyes!

"Opening a memory box is like stepping into a time machine, it takes you back to the moments that made you who you are."

Chapter 18 - Babymoon

As the time grew shorter until we met baby girl, we were busy 'nesting', I cleaned the house at least 3 times a day, rearranged the newly painted pink nursery at least 12 times and had begun to wash the never-ending laundry. There was only 8 weeks to go until our due date, we were so excited to finally have her here with us! We tossed around a few names but couldn't decide on just one so we decided to wait until we met her and knew it'd just come to us then.

We had spent the last year saving our asses off, other than moms holiday and the chocolate fountain, we didn't do anything fancy!

That is until Jay decided to surprise me with ticking the last big item off my list! A cruise! Yes, I know it's crazy to do a huge cruise so close to my due date. But the idea of a babymoon sounded great!

Just Jay & I, for probably the last time for a couple of years! We booked a cruise to France, it was short but now that I was waddling instead of walking, I think it suited just fine. We had a balcony room, overlooking the sea, the boat had everything you could wish for, from pizza bars to water slides to concerts, it really had it all! I loved it! We spent those 3 days in a complete love bubble; savouring this time together before we came a trio! We docked in Calais, grabbed a Croissant, an Iced Chocolate and of course a magnet, before heading back to the boat.

We started the journey home with 3 more days to spend together, we took it easy, casual walks around the deck, cuddled on the deckchairs, ate the amazing food and had some early nights watching movies. I couldn't ask for more!

We arrived back, collected Lily from my Moms house and met, Mike, the Irish man my mom was talking to. He was lovely, he was warm, easy to talk to and he was even excited for baby to get here! Jay and Mike went out the back talking guy talk, while me and Mom sat and exchanged notes on Mike. She was in love, I could see it already, but I also know how much easier it is in that generation, if there's feelings, they aren't afraid to speak their mind, they don't have Instagram or Facebook to go stalking the exes and they simply don't care about it anyway. She explained how they called most days and they already have another meet up planned! I was so excited for her!!

We got home, threw our feet up, spent some time with Lily and I turned back on my chocolate fountain! 21 year old Georgia really had some great ideas, this thing saved me throughout my pregnancy. The next few weeks were tough, I was called into the hospital twice with Braxton Hicks (false labour, who came up with that!!). I was really sick near the end and was in a lot of pain. I spent the last week in bed with Lily while Jay finished up work. He had just begun his leave, when that night at 38 weeks, my waters broke while I was catching whatever broken sleep I could!

"Babymoon: Where relaxation meets anticipation, and every moment together becomes a cherished memory"

Chapter 19 - She's here!

Labour was, let's say, eventful!

Jay was in the room with me being so supportive. I huffed, puffed, screamed, cried, got sick and everything in between.

After 8 hours of labour, she was finally here, our perfect 8lb 2oz baby girl, Arabella, or Bella for short. It was one of our top names and as soon as we met her, we just knew it was meant for her!

It's true when people say, once she's there you won't feel a thing! I had 2 doctors sewing up my hoo-ha and I didn't even bat an eyelid. I was in my baby bubble and nothing was ruining this moment! Jay left the room to call our Moms, once he left, I lay her on my legs, she sat for ages just looking into my eyes, while I was lost in hers too! She was so beautiful, absolutely perfect and the image of me when I was a baby. She had my eyes, Jays nose and mouth and she had my blonde hair.

Naturally, this moment brought up a lot of emotions. I don't think many people talk about the heartbreak you feel for many reasons, even though it's such a happy moment, all I could think of were 2 things...

Our angel baby, would they have looked exactly like her? They would've been nearly 3 now, a fully grown toddler. I looked at Bella, wondering all about her older sibling. The other thought that spun around my head was pure fear! She wasn't inside me anymore, she was out in this big bad world, I couldn't protect her as much as I have been these last 9 months, what do we even do with a baby? Of course I read hundreds of books with loads of information, but the second she's in your arms, you forget everything! I was already panicking about the first diaper, the first bath, putting her onto solid foods! She was here 15minutes and instead of feeling all this love and bonding with her, I was panicking so much I couldn't hold her anymore!

I called Jay, he came in to see me bawling my eyes out and having a panic attack. He freaked and called the nurses to make sure I was ok. The nurses came in, advised Jay to sit with me while they took Bella to the nursery.

I couldn't catch my breath, I just kept crying and crying, eventually I think I passed out, I don't remember a thing after that. I woke up a couple of hours later to Jay asleep on the armchair, holding my hand. I felt numb, no emotions were registering in my brain at all. I didn't get it, I was so excited to meet her, now my perfect girl was there and I couldn't even enjoy it?

It was time for the first feed, Jay picked her up from the nursery, transferred her to me and I spent 10 minutes trying to get her to latch. I was just getting frustrated constantly and I didn't want to hurt her if I lashed out. You could see Jay was worried, he couldn't understand it either and I'm sure he was worried for the both of us. She eventually finished her feed; Jay laid her on his chest and burped her until she fell asleep again. He was a natural, he took to her perfectly and she loved him, why couldn't I bond like that?!

We got discharged from the hospital the next day but they had arranged a councillor to visit our house once a week to check up on me. I hated counselling, we tried it during our roommate phase and immediately quit, I went through it a lot when dad left, as a child with a horrible therapist I think this set me up to hate it for life! A couple days went by, no sleep was had, my moods were up and down, me and Jay were sleeping in separate rooms and we didn't speak in days. Eventually the first counselling session came by. I was dreading it, "yes miss I know my life is shit, anything else you'd like to tell me" I muttered to myself mockingly once I heard the doorbell ring.

"Hey Momma, I'm Jill, how are you doing!" She said in her chirpy voice, and "momma" really?! I couldn't wait for her to leave! I tried to hide the fact I felt horrible, let on everything was going great!

Typical therapist saw straight through me, she could probably feel the tension in the house, never mind the state of the place at the time! "Clear Space, Clear Mind" and all that bullshit!

Eventually, I gave up putting on this show, I couldn't do it anymore, I was too tired to fake it. "It's fucking shit ok, I'm shit, the baby's sleep is shit, the house is shit, my relationship is shit, everything's fucking shit!!" I lashed out! Jay poked his head around the corner, pretty sure he was making sure 'Chirpy Jill' was ok. I just woke the baby up, great! I felt horrible, I knew I wasn't doing a good enough job of being a Mom or a Wife right now and I genuinely did feel so ashamed of myself for it, I just wanted out!

Jill continued to ask stupid questions, "do you have any thoughts of harming yourself or others Mrs. Rogers?", the only person I wanted to harm right now was her, nosey bitch, sticking her nose into other people's business! "No, I don't ok! Are we done here?" I snapped. She agreed to end the session and reschedule for next week again. Just as she was finally walking out the door, she handed me some leaflets "PPD information for Mothers" it said on the front cover.

I slammed the door and dropped to the floor in tears. Jay picked up the leaflets and just held me as long as I needed.

"I'm so sorry" I cried, snotting all over his baby sick filled T-shirt! "Shhh, you're ok" he said, rocking me like a child.

That was it, I'm not crazy, it's Postpartum Depression, I was just one of the unlucky ones who had it ruin the first week with my daughter. I was determined to get back to myself, I needed to be there for Bella but I also needed to be there for Jay, he had taken this whole new dad thing on, practically all by himself, all while dealing with me!

"A Daughter is a little girl who grows up to be a friend" - Unknown

Chapter 20 - Guess I'm trying to find myself again!

I woke the next morning, had about 3 hours of broken sleep, Bella definitely doesn't take after her Mom in the sleep department anyway! She woke every single hour, wanting to be rocked or fed or burped, it was never ending!

I thought you were supposed to enjoy these newborn days? How is it this hard, and why does nobody talk about it honestly?

Today was the first day I didn't wake up like a demon! That reassurance that I wasn't going crazy, may have just saved my life. We broke out the stroller, strapped Bella in, attached Lily's lead and braved the outdoors for the first time. I wasn't ready for visitors yet so neither of our Moms had even met Arabella yet, I felt like a monster but I didn't want them to see the state I was in!

I opened the door, the fresh air hit my face and it was amazing, part of my felt alive again. For the first time since Bella was born, I smiled. Jay teared up, put his arm around me and says "you got this G, you can make it through anything!". With that we began our walk, watching the world go by, children running on the sand, dogs swimming in the sea and I thought to myself, this is actually what I've always wanted. A loving husband, our own dog and pushing a stroller with our beautiful baby girl, along the beach. I could see the light at the end of the tunnel.

I stopped isolating myself from people, called Mom and invited her over to meet her first granddaughter. As soon as she walked through the door, the tears started again and I ran to her for a hug. She stroked my hair like she used to when I was upset as a child, patted my back and whispered "I'm proud of you Georgia, you did it, you have got this, I believe in you!". I smiled while wiping the tears from my cheeks. I needed that, there's something about that reassurance from your Mom that just solves everything.

Jay came into the room with Bella and placed her in Moms arms. She sat, analysing her beauty for ages, just soaking up the newborn feels. "She looks just like you Georgia, it feels like I'm transported back 30 years ago with you in my arms!". "Jay scoffed, she actually has my nose and mouth thank you very much!" he laughed. Mom and I looked at each other and said "Yeah the poor thing!" The whole room burst out with laughter. "I'm kidding Jason, congratulations, I hear you are a natural! I'm so glad my Georgia ended up with someone like you!" said Mom while holding his hand.

Jay caught my eye, we smiled at each other with pride, he winked at me as if to say "We got this!".

Mom stayed for a few days to help clean and feed, she was just amazing! Days go by with visitors passing through, falling in love with Bella and some of them really made me realise, my real friends. Some work "friends" came by, barged passed me, held Bella and left without a hug, a congrats, a check in or a helping hand.

Others didn't even bother Bella, they let her sleep, dropped over some meals, even volunteered to do our washing! They were our real friends.

One morning we heard a knock on the door, we looked through the peep hole but we couldn't work out who it was! "Hellloooo Lovebirds, I know you're in there!" she called out in a strong Irish accent. It was Megan, I couldn't believe it! I hadn't seen her in over a year! I hear congratulations are in order! She grabbed my hand, "how are you doing girl" she asked, once again like the emotional wreck I was, I burst out in tears, "I'm so sorry Megan, I completely lost contact, I've just been so distra-" Megan cut me off mid-sentence, "Shhhh, don't worry about it, I'm here now aren't I? And you have a lot on your plate girl!"

I loved that girl with all my heart, Jay loved her too! She chilled out on the sofa with us for the evening, we talked all evening, in between feeds and naps and diaper changes that is, but that's life now. A new amazing chapter had begun and I have the people I love most around me.

"I m so sorry, I've been so caught up in telling you all my stories I forgot to ask, how's your boyfriend nowadays?" I ask, Megan just bursts out laughing and replied "Oh girl, long gone, this woman isn't settling for anyone, I'm still travelling around, having one night stands here and there, with absolutely no responsibilities! Husbands and babies are just not my idea of a happy life, no offence! Yours are cute and all but personally, not for me! Of course, I got an earful from Mammy but I'm sure she'll get over it! I don't want to follow the norms of 'womanhood', this woman does it different and I'm proud of it!"

I just smiled, gave her a hug "and cheers to that!" we said while we quietly clinked our Champagne flutes, filled with Sprite! I was so proud of Megan for following her own path, not being afraid to live differently from most people and most of all, I was proud she wasn't afraid to say "fuck off" to people who had anything to say about it! Her new motto was "Don't take advise from someone you wouldn't switch places with!".

Megan left after 2 days, Mom had moved back to her place and Jay was acting very suspicious. He had been 'popping out to the shops' every hour or so and was very cagey when I pointed out the fact, he's not coming back with anything?

Anyway, I left Bella with him while I went for a run, I was never a runner but I found it amazing to clear my head, switch off from Mom and just be Georgia again!

I got home to an empty house, what was going on? I just left 1 hour ago and they've disappeared! I went upstairs to check the room and was greeted by a note that read..

"Get changed, feel sexy and meet me at the Beachfront Bar P.S, check the wardrobe ... Jason x"

Oh god, I haven't felt sexy in a long time, but I walked to the wardrobe to find this amazing silver mini dress, I haven't worn a mini dress since my party days, will this even fit?! My boobs had doubled in size, my hips were massive and in my opinion I still looked pregnant. As I got undressed, I thought to myself, it's time to stop avoiding the mirror. I didn't look at myself naked since before Bella, I couldn't face it, I felt shit so I just assumed I looked shit too! I take off each layer, one by one, each revealing more stretch marks, cellulite and 'flab' underneath. I was just about to throw a tantrum and have a mental breakdown but I thought back to 25 year old me, who decided to change her view of herself and focus on the positives!

I traced my stretch marks with my finger, each one representing the work my amazing body did to grow my healthy baby girl. The 'flab' I refer to, was her home and the cellulite, let's face it everyone has cellulite! A smile grew on my face once again, all it took is that one split second of rethinking my reaction to change how my night would go.

What was even going on? Why was I getting so done up? I slipped on the dress, and I do have to say, I looked fucking sexy, I was a sexy Mom, I was a sexy wife and Georgia is god damn sexy! I paired the dress with some heels, big earrings and I took my time doing my hair and makeup, as a mom, time to yourself to do your hair and makeup was valuable, I barely had time to shower these last couple of days, never mind get glam!

I text Jay, told him I was on my way. I stepped outside the door into the Uber and arrived to the Beachfront Bar like he asked. I rang him, no answer. I was starting to feel my palms getting sweaty. I hadn't gone somewhere myself in a long time, but I wasn't letting all my hard work go to waste! I opened the door to the bar, checked out the back and then eventually I heard music, "is that high school musical?" I thought to myself, this small pub on the outskirts of Edinburgh, surely isn't playing my favourite playlist? I opened the doors to where the music was coming from....

"Surprise!!!! Happy 30th Birthday Georgia!!!" all my closest family and friends had planned this amazing party for me! I forgot my own birthday, but who can blame me with everything going on!

I looked through the centre of the room, saw my beautiful Husband who had worked so hard all day to pull this off and my perfect Bella. My life was complete. I had everything I wanted, I ruled out all the What Ifs and it paid off!

Megan had stuck around to surprise me, Mom was there with her new boyfriend Mike! Jays family came, some of the girls from work arrived. I may have had a small circle, but the people in it were amazing, they were my world!

Once the hellos where done, Jay pulled me aside and whispered "Holy fuck G, you just turned 30, just had

baby and you still look like my favourite dessert!", I
smiled, winked and him and said "Dessert comes after
the party babe, I wouldn't fill up on cake if I were you!".
I felt like I could take on the world again, I danced to
my favourite songs with Bella, sang my heart out with
Megan and had to redo the karaoke night with Jay.

"Start of something New - Troy and Gabriella" appeared
on the screen. We grabbed the mics and more than
likely once again, slaughtered the song, but we didn't
care! Everyone in that room loved our authentic selves
and we couldn't be happier!

"One final thing before the night ends" announced Jay.
"You wrote this list 9 years ago, grew into an amazing
woman, wife and Mom since then. You may have only
found it again 5 months ago but you still smashed it
and never let 21 year old Georgia down!" We reassessed
the list and saw one remaining goal - Make it to 30!
Ticked it off the list and celebrated once again!

"Finding yourself is not really how it works. You aren't a £10 note in last winters coat pocket. You are also not lost. Your true self is right there, buried under cultural conditioning, other peoples opinions and inaccurate conclusions you drew as a kid that became your beliefs about who you are. Finding yourself is actually returning to yourself. An unlearning, an excavation, a remembering of who you were before the world got its hands on you."

Chapter 21 - Mom

"Mama" Bella mumbles from her bouncer.

Her first word, my new name for the rest of her life.

Yeah I was her Mom since she was conceived, but I had never been called Mom by her yet. This was bittersweet, my baby girl is growing so quick, she said her first word already! But at the same time my identity has changed again, I respond to Mom now, a generic word that most women are labelled with in their lifetime.

Don't get me wrong, I love being a Mom, but this seems to be the only thing that summarises me at the moment. I was part of a 'Mom' group, had Mom friends. I felt like I wasn't Georgia anymore!

"Here we go again" I sighed as I sat staring at my laptop with "Finding Me" blinking on an empty document. I was scared to speak to anyone about how I was feeling, was it selfish? Was it ungrateful? I felt like the most horrible person on the planet and that I was the only one going through this!

I started typing, the words began to flow. I put every thought that entered my mind, down on that word document. I typed and typed, feeling like I was in my own world it was amaz- *baby cries* back to reality. I get up, do a feed, burp her and sit Bella on my lap. Straight away the words began to flow again. This is it; this is my outlet. Eventually, Jay came home from work. I was 6 pages deep in thoughts about Motherhood.

I stepped away from the desk, kissed Jay hello and began to prepare dinner. As dinner was just about ready, I popped my head through the living room door to call for Jay. He was sat reading my laptop, a tear rolled down his face as he glanced up at me. "Is this how you really feel G?" He asks shakily. Oh no, this is where he says I'm an ungrateful bitch and that I shouldn't be thinking like that, I thought to myself.

I just stood there in silence with my head hanging low. "This is amazing G, you have to help other parents out with this, write a book, write a weekly newsletter, something, anything! But you have to do it, this is so raw, authentic, brave and I think it'll save people's lives" he said.

I couldn't believe it!

It was ok to feel this way? It'll save lives? Maybe I'm not the only one to think like this! "Really?" I asked nervously.

"Of course!"

This was it the best of both worlds! I could be an amazing Mom, at home with my baby, all while using writing as my own little therapy session, which also helps other parents in the long run!

I spent the next couple of days researching book writing and how to start a newsletter. Eventually I came across a well-known publisher looking for local authors to submit their stories. I looked at the requirements and immediately began writing every day, during feeds, while Bella napped, even made voice notes when something came to me on my run. I was on a roll, I may have just found my purpose!

"Being a Mother is learning about strengths you didn't know you had and dealing with fears you didn't know existed"

- Linda Wooten

Chapter 22 - An Author

I may have only established what I want to do at the age of 30, but that was ok, I wasn't ready for this opportunity when I was younger, I didn't have the knowledge i have now. For the first time in months I was excited to see what was to come!

I compiled the first 3 chapters, wrote a summary and a bit about myself and sent it off to the publishers. When the part came about writing everything about me, I included everything, the PPD, the breakdown in my relationship, my miscarriage, everything. I wanted to be completely honest and hopefully resonate with other parents that were feeling the same.

A few days passed, the day came for my skydive and I was buzzing! I don't know what it was but this new lease of life since finding my purpose, was amazing! Jay and I were finally back to acting like a married couple, of course a few arguments here and there but we laughed, danced and cuddled, something we hadn't done in a while.

Jay dropped me to the door and drove to the landing zone. I walked in, got suited up and listened to the safety briefing. The walk to the plane is when the nerves hit but I still couldn't wait to do this!!

We boarded the plane, strapped up to our instructors and watched each person disappear out of the sliding door one by one. I was the last one waiting to jump. We slid to the door, our legs dangling 10,000ft in the air. The instructor put my head on his chest, counted "1...2..." and jumped, he didn't get to 3, they said they never go to 3 because that's when people tend to grab onto something! It was happening, I was falling through the sky at nearly 200mph! The fear left my body after the initial drop, it turned to complete amazement and pride. The point of maximum danger was the point of minimum fear. I spent so long ruling out the What ifs that it didn't even enter my head "what if the parachute doesn't open" "what if I don't make it" - it didn't matter, I was doing it, there was no going back and everything went perfectly! It was the most amazing experience of my life!

We touched down, I ran to Jay and Bella, hugged them and dropped to my knees.

"I fucking did it! Fuck you, fear!" I shouted, looking up to the sky, not even registering what had just happened.

I've been through so much, and I'm still here standing the proudest I've ever been!

I got home, hung my certificate up on the wall and busied myself until I heard back from the publisher.

Jay walks through the door one day after work, with a small box, tied together with a red ribbon. I looked at him filled with curiosity as he handed me the package. I untied the ribbon slowly, opened the box and was greeted with a name plaque that read...

Georgia Rogers - Published Author

He had so much faith in me, it pushed me to believe it myself!

The publishers advised they received my submission and would be in touch within 4 to 6 weeks.

I continued to write, chapter after chapter, saving it all as I went along, hoping but the time they got back to me I would be at least half way there.

The day came around, an email pinged on my phone. I couldn't face it, I threw my phone across the sofa and had a cup of tea to calm my nerves. Eventually, knowing I had to face it at some point, I opened the email desperately searching for the outcome through all the other legal bits.

Denied.

My heart sank, immediately burst into tears, of course I didn't get it! It's just my luck, who do I think I am trying to preach about motherhood when I know so little!

Straight away, my mind went into a deep dark hole of negative thoughts and I was ready to give up. I threw down my phone and had a solo pity party all afternoon until Jay got home.

"How's the writing going? Any word yet?" He asked. "Just forget it!" I snap back at him, showing him the email.

"G, you're stronger than this, these guys in fancy suits in their little office don't have a clue how big this book

148

is gonna be. There are hundreds of other publishers, you have it all compiled now so just send it off to a few others and I guarantee you you'll be picking which deal you want in the next few weeks"

He was right, that was just one group of people who didn't like what I had. I am better than that. This book is needed, a raw and honest insight into motherhood! Yes, I know it's a bit of a taboo subject but it needs to be heard! I sat up, grabbed my laptop and hit send to 5 more publishers.

In the meantime, I began a social media platform to gain some audience. I posted about the behind the scenes of book writing, as a first time mom and some snippets of the book! Overnight my following grew to over 10,000 people! I woke up to hundreds of messages thanking me for being so honest and practically saving their lives, they too thought they were this horrible ungrateful monster and thought they were all alone.

Writing was my new outlet, it helped me as well as others, I offloaded my thoughts into a newsletter each week, receiving amazing feedback each time!

One day, I received a message on my Instagram page, asking for my email. I was sceptical but continued 'ruling out the what ifs' and sent them my email. "What

if it's a troubled mom? What if it's a Publisher?" I
thought to myself.

The next day, an email came through. I read the first
three lines as they appeared in my phone notifications.

"Hi there, thank you so much for providing your email
through your Instagram platform. We are Keatings...."

It cut off there, I was so intrigued, thank goodness
there's no read receipts on emails!

I clicked onto the notification, opening the entirety of
the email. They continued to introduce themselves as
"Keatings Publishers", one of my videos had gone viral
on TikTok and loved my work. They attached a
document to top the email, I opened it expecting their
logo or some legal bullshit, but no, it was an offer
letter!

They proposed a 6 figure, 2 book deal! I didn't even
submit my book yet. They only read the snippets and
still send me an offer! I couldn't believe it, I waited for
Jay to come home to tell him the news and just as he

walked through the door, 2 more offers came through from the other publishers!

It's crazy to think if I let that first publishers' decision sway me off my decision and didn't have Jay to talk me into keep going. This never would have happened!

The offers continued to roll in over the next week, some requesting 2 books, some requesting 5 and some even asked me to do a tour!

I sat down with Jay, weighed out the options and went for the best one. We went with "Torc Publishers". Torc was the name of the waterfall I visited in Ireland when I first started this amazing journey of me, it hit home straight away and I knew this was the right one! It was 3 books, a tour around the UK & Ireland and a 7 figure cheque at the end of it! This is life changing!!

The next day, I had a Zoom meeting with the publishers themselves, we talked about the target audience, timescales and all things business. I asked them about the tour and discussed that I am a Mom too so I cannot be gone for long. They completely understood and were with me through every step.

The pressure was on, time to get Book Number 1 published and out on the shelves! I announced the news to my socials and received an amazing response. Here I was, with a huge book deal, about to go on tour. All with this little idea that stemmed from writing, my main form of therapy.

Being an author was never something that entered any of my 'Future Plans' that I sat around writing, only to throw away or forget about them a couple of months later. This really taught me, no matter how much you try to plan things, you have a life path, the universe knows what you need and what you deserve and what's for you won't pass you!

I met Jay when I wasn't looking for a partner and now became an author without really trying.

I did have a couple of months, while I was finishing the book, that I felt like an imposter. How did I deserve this? Some people make it their life's mission to try and become an author, and it never happens for them, but I'm sat here with nearly 300,000 followers on Instagram and this life changing opportunity all of a sudden?

My life's purpose did a complete 360 in the space of a couple of hours. I went from crying, panicking about being a shit Mom, just after overcoming PPD, to sharing my raw story of my experience and it becoming something huge.

I celebrated the day I completed the book, Jay, Bella, Megan, Mom and Mike all came around our place for a dinner party. I felt so loved, so supported and so optimistic for the future!

"Cheers to Georgia and whatever comes next!" They shouted.

"And to ruling out the What Ifs" I added, everyone laughed and cheered again!

"Writing is the painting of the voice"

- Voltaire

"Writing is the painting of the voice"

- Voltaire

Chapter 23 - It's Go Time

The book was finished, edited and the cover was designed. I was holding a physical hardback copy of my own book in my hands?!

I often think, if I didn't go through that horrible experience of losing myself, feeling crazy and even feeling like giving up on life, I wouldn't be in this position. It was a bittersweet experience, I didn't know who I was and I lost the first week with Bella, but I came out with this opportunity? I couldn't quite wrap my head around it.

I felt guilty, should something so horrible, really change my life for the best? Should I be making money from fucking up the bond with my baby.

I had to remind myself, this book was a therapy outlet for me and if my social media platforms are anything to go by, it'll hopefully save people's lives who are going through the same thing.

My first launch, I travelled back to London for the event. Once again, I sat at Victoria Train Station, looking back on how far I have come. The bookstore I was launching at was about a 10 minute walk from my old flat. This is where it all began, that one decision to change my life. I remember sitting in my tiny bedroom, looking down on all the people who "had their life together" thinking it would never be me.

Admittedly, I don't have my life together, I don't think anyone does. But, I know 25 year old Georgia would be so proud of who I was now.

I continued the walk to the bookstore, I probably should have caught an Uber to save my freshly styled hair but I needed time to think and reflect on what's going on. I arrived 30 minutes early, greeted by - me? A big sign with my face on it stood tall at the front door. I always wanted my face on a poster but seeing it now, not so much! Self judgment aside, I couldn't believe how many chairs were there. A podium at the top of the room with copies of my book scattered around the store. I actually had to pinch myself, "this really is my life" I thought to myself.

Shortly the people began to fill the seats, each one with a copy of the book under their arm. "Oh my god, there are strangers, with my writing, technically my therapy journal, they are actually reading it!". I knew I had support online but the book only launched this morning and as that thought entered my head, the shop assistant tapped me on my shoulder, waking me from my daydream.

"Excuse me, Miss Rogers?" she said, as her face lit up red like a tomato. "You can call me Georgia, is everything alright?" I replied.

"My manager just asked me to advise you your book has completely sold out" she said excitedly. "That's the quickest sell out we have ever had!" she adds!

I was speechless. I'm pretty sure we offloaded 1,000 copies here this morning, and they're all sold out?? Oh Lordy, I'm suddenly a lot more nervous!

"I'm not supposed to ask, but is there any chance we could get a picture Mrs - Georgia?" The girl whispers. "With me? Really? I mean yeah, if you want my head in your camera roll, then why not?" I laugh.

"You're literally the talk of the college campus, everyone I know follows you and you've inspired so many people to find out what they really want instead of following the college 'norms'. They're 'ruling out the what ifs' I suppose" she grinned as she takes her picture!

157

I am actually helping people, real life people. I peek through the curtain, the room is packed. The queue was out the door. Just as I felt like I was going to get sick, the store manager pushed me through the curtains and onto the stage.

"It's show time" I thought to myself, putting on a brave face.

"Good Afternoon Ladies & Gentlemen, I am amazed by this turnout and I just want to thank you all so much for your support. Some of you may have been following the book journey online and others may have just been walking past the store and hopefully I caught your eye!

I just want to preface, you see me up here, styled by an amazing team, walking around in my high heels, probably looking super comfortable up here. Well I'm always honest with you guys, I spent all of yesterday in my husbands T-shirt and boxers, a pair of fluffy socks, hair in a messy bun, covered in Bellas sick and shit. And I'm pretty sure I nearly shit myself coming on this stage." The audience laughed, it broke the silence, I was already more comfortable. But what I said was completely true. I want people to relate to me, not think oh god, she writes all this and then looks like that. After a great chat, a couple of questions, reading a couple of pages and hearing people's stories, I genuinely just cried on stage. "Don't worry guys I'm not having another breakdown." I laughed. "I just can't believe so many people feel this way and it took me to write this book, to get the conversation going. We feel so alone in these situations and are so horrible to ourselves so I'm glad we've created this lovely community we can count on and know we are never alone in this". I ended the show on that note and left the stage.

The first show was done, the shop had sold out and photographers from all over London were getting pictures from every angle! I took one more glance at the crowd, a few of the book critics had begun their TikTok videos reviewing the event and people began to queue to get their books signed at the opposite end of the room. I had a chat with every single person that came up to me, hearing their stories and being able to check in with them was amazing. Suddenly I notice a familiar face, Emma? Is that you? My stomach hit the floor.

I haven't seen her in over 5 years. She still looks the exact same. "Hey G" she says with her head hanging low. Initially I was pissed off, I didn't want to see her, she was a nobody to me. She completely abandoned me when I needed her most. Emotions took over, I saw she needed a hug, I got up wrapped my arms around her and said "Grab a coffee after eh?". Her face lit up, you could tell she wasn't expecting it at all. And to be honest neither was I.

I finished up with the signing and met Emma, standing by the front door. "Any recommendations Londoner?" I laugh, trying to break the ice. She points at the cafe next door. We grabbed a table, ordered our drinks and finally began to talk. "What have you been up to Em?" "Nothing, absolutely nothing. I'm the exact same as when you last saw me, except this time I'm a single Mom to be." She lifts back her jacket to reveal a bump.

"Congratulations!" I say awkwardly, she clearly wasn't excited but what else was I supposed to say? We weren't close enough to say "Oh shit" and I didn't fancy going to my next tour day with a black eye either. "I mean thanks, it definitely wasn't planned though, it was a one night stand and the dad ghosted me as soon as he heard the news" she added.

"Ah shit, I'm sorry Em"

"No I'm fucking sorry Georgia, I was so fucking jealous you had the balls to leave that shithole of a job and go on the search for happiness. I watched your Instagram stories in Thailand and then I couldn't do it anymore, you had the life I wanted, the handsome boyfriend, now husband, the memories, the house and the dog" "Yeah you have the baby too, but you know that was never in the plans for me so I wasn't exactly jealous of that part" she laughed.

"Emma, yeah it was shitty, you left when I really needed you, but it's 5 years later. Trust me, once you read that book, you'll realise I don't have my shit together." I tried to reassure her.

"I've been following you for the past year G, I just didn't have the courage to add you under my own name, not that you'd notice my name pop up amongst 250,000 others but I just didn't want to risk it! I've felt horrible for years but I still never had the balls to reach out to you, that is until I started to read the snippets of your book you used to post. I began thinking about ruling out the what ifs, what if I text her and she actually replies, or what if I text her and she completely ignores me? I needed to find out and I thought it'd be easier to blend into a big group here and hopefully bump into you that way" she says, followed by a sigh of relief, it's like that was sitting on her chest for ages!

I didn't really know what to say, part of me wanted to hug her and have my bestie back but the other part of me was stubborn, still hurt and couldn't really be arsed listening to this drama at the ripe age of 30!

"Let's leave it at that then eh?" I said quietly.

"We've cleared the air, I'm happy to move on if you are." I said, Emma's face dropped, I don't think she was expecting me to respond like that. "Well in reality Em, I needed you in a tough time, you were supposed to be there hyping me up and be proud of me but instead you got jealous and completely left me".

If this was 25 year old Georgia, I would've said ok and continued to just be friends with her but after all this work I've done for myself, I wasn't letting someone back into my life that doesn't benefit me. I felt like a bitch but I knew it was the right decision.

"Ok then, I guess I'll see you when I see you Georgia" she said with her head hanging low as she walked away.

"Life begins
at the end of
your comfort
zone"
- Neale
Donald Walsh

Chapter 24 - A Whirlwind

The book launches and tours kept coming, I was speaking all over the UK. I loved being able to connect with my readers and listening to their feedback and even their own stories. It felt amazing that they trusted me enough to confide in.

Between each tour I came home, spent time with Bella and Jay and soaked up the moments with them. Bella was growing so quick! She was walking, talking and she had her own little personality. Jay and I were closer than ever. We enjoyed our time together when I was home, he was always my cheerleader when it came to my writing and the tours.

My next tour was to Ireland! I couldn't wait! The place where I found myself, got engaged and my second home in a way.

I decided Bella was finally big enough to bring with me and I always wanted to bring my family to Killarney so we might as well all go together! I packed our bags, Jay took some time off and booked the flights.

I was so excited yet so nervous, bringing Bella on her first flight! We arrived to the airport, stood on the escalator and when we reached the top, who was there only Mom! Jay had arranged her to come with us too, she was still visiting Mike so it tied in perfectly for us all to go together! Mom was such a help on the flight with Bella. We kept her entertained the whole way and touched down in Cork.

You know that burst of heat when you land in a foreign country and they open the cabin doors and you just feel pure bliss? Ireland gave me that same feeling but of course with colder weather! The air was so fresh and the fields so green.

We got our luggage, grabbed a taxi to Cork city and checked into a hotel, as I had a book launch the next morning in a local bookstore. I only ever ran through Cork city when I was trying to catch the bus to Killarney so it was nice to have some time here to explore. We walked along the Main Street, grabbed some lunch, listened to a street performer and had an early night with some dinner delivered to the room.

The next morning, I was getting ready to go to the bookstore, when in the corner of my eye, I spot Bella in the most beautiful little pink dress alongside Jay looking as handsome as ever in his shirt and jeans. "You two are looking very snazzy" I said with a grin on my face.

"Oh we're just going to see this ol' sell out author in a bookstore in the city" he laughed. "We wouldn't miss this for the world, Bella gets to finally see what a rockstar her momma is" he said wrapping his arms around me.

I was so excited to have my family there with me. The people who made this book possible. We went downstairs to leave the hotel. Mom was standing at the front door also waiting to come with us and around the corner came Mike. He had travelled up from Killarney to see me too! I practically skipped to the bookstore, invited my family up onto the stage at the end and I was beaming from ear to ear by the end of it.

We had our celebratory lunch, jumped in the car and drove down with Mike to Killarney. While I sat in the back with my own little family, I had a bittersweet thought.

Mom was finally happy driving around with Mikes hand laid gently on her lap, her daughter and her grandchild sat in the back having a singsong. Mike was there to support not only her, but me too! This made me think of Dad. He left years ago now, but I kind of wish he was there supporting me, spending time with Bella and meeting Jay. I wonder if he had seen my book, my name was changed now so maybe he hasn't even realised it was me! I secretly shed a tear in the back seat, facing out the window, pretending to admire the views. I don't get away with much in front of Jay though, it's like he can read my mind. He put his hand on my shoulder and said we'll chat later.

I cleaned myself up, arrived to the hotel and said goodbye to Mom and Mike who had a place just up the road. Once again, I walked through the doors to the hotel, greeted by the same receptionist as the other two times I had stayed here.

"No way, is that really you Ms. Williams? - I mean Mrs. Rogers" she laughed. I loved how it really felt like coming home when I got here. They remembered my name and I was greeted with a huge hug!

"Goodness, each time you walk through these doors you have just excelled more and more in life! And I see you've added a new little addition to the family" she smiled.

"I've been reading your book Mrs. Rogers, I wish I had something like this when I was having my 2 girls!".

I couldn't believe it, I don't think it had registered in my head that my book was actually selling out everywhere, there was reviews online, it was launched all over the UK and Ireland and people actually have it in their homes!

"Thanks so much, call me Georgia by the way! And this is Jason and Arabella" I replied.

She showed us to our room. The beautiful lake view just like before! I took a couple of minutes to sit and reflect on the balcony. I remembered the time I sat here crying my eyes out, not knowing what to do, all by myself. Now I looked behind me to see Jay putting Bella to bed and on his way to join me outside. I really had come a long way!

Jay put his hand on my shoulder once again and asked what was up in the car. I kind of tried to sway away from the question a few times but I knew he would be able to help and it wouldn't do me any good to keep it bottled up.

I told him my feelings about my Dad and just began to cry. I never really spoke about Dad and I don't think I've dealt with him leaving either so when I do think about it, it all comes out and I end up in tears. Jay listened to it all, let me cry and explained how my feelings were totally valid. He too, had his dad walk out on him at a young age. He explained how he missed out on 'guy things', how to shave, how to talk to girls, how to fix a car. But he looks back now and sees he can still do it all.

"You didn't think twice about clearing the air with Emma, but at the same time, you had respect for yourself enough not to let her back in as she didn't benefit your life at all. She left and it was her loss, right?" He said. "Well try and do the same thing with your Dad, I know you can't exactly clear the air with him but I'm sure we could try something".

I cuddled into him, feeling a lot better and just watched the sun go down that evening.

The next day was the book launch, Bella had been teething so she was very grumpy today so we couldn't bring her along. Mom was happy to look after her for the day so myself and Jay went about the day, ourselves. The event was at 2pm, we had breakfast and dropped Bella off all by 9am so we said we would fill the time with a bit of an adventure. We walked through the National Park, past the curious deer, along the river and underneath the huge trees until we reached Ross Castle and the lake that surrounded it. It was still relatively early and I could see Jay light up as if he just had the worlds best idea! He grabbed my hand, without telling

169

me a thing and ran to the furthest away point of the lane surrounding the river. "Do it" he said. As if I was already in on this great plan of his and knew exactly what to do.

"Do what exactly?" I laughed.

"Just scream, let everything out! Say what you want to say to your Dad, whatever feels right" he said excitedly.

I did exactly that, I screamed and screamed and cried and cried some more but I felt fucking amazing after it! I know no one could hear me, but it was out there, it was off my chest and I felt free!

We laughed the whole way back to the town centre. "Thanks babe, I really needed that. As silly as it sounds you knew exactly what to do!" I said swinging arms like a little child. I got ready, smashed another book launch, met some amazing people and joined Mom, Mike and Bella at a local restaurant for dinner.

"This trip has been amazing. It may have originally been for work but I just want to thank you all for all your support and I want to say a huge welcome to the family to Mike." Mom and Mike looked at me with a shocked look on their faces, squeezed each others hands and started beaming from ear to ear for the rest of the evening.

We caught our flight home the next morning, said goodbye to Mike for a while and returned back to normal life after all the shows were done.

"The moment you accept responsibility for everything in your life, is the moment you gain the power to change anything in your life" - Hal Elrod

Chapter 25 - Back to Reality

Bellas first birthday was approaching, this last year had been crazy! It was filled with battling postpartum depression, having to find myself again as a Mom, turning 30, jumping out of a plane, writing my first book, touring around the UK & Ireland, closing things off with Emma and welcoming Mike into the family.

There was lots of ups and downs, but we made it out of it together. It was lovely having time to spend together again, watching Bella grow into such an amazing little girl. Jays business was booming and I was beginning to write my second book.

I was wrapping Bellas presents, crying about how quick the year went by, how I was so busy, I barely made any memories with her. I had 'mom guilt' as they call it. I spent so much time working on myself, focusing on success, which was all to benefit the family in my mind. But in reality, I missed out on a lot, Jay took on minding Bella all the times I was away, I missed her first steps and we didn't have one proper family picture together.

I sat with Jay, explaining to him how I felt. He reminded me that it s ok to be "selfish", yes, of course your children come first but, you need to feel good and be your best self in order for your children to thrive and have a good role model. He was right, as always! If I didn't work on myself and build this amazing community of women, I would probably still be stuck in that same rut of having postpartum depression, no direction and feeling lost with this new identity as Mom.

Now, Bella has a strong, successful and happy Mom to look up to, a great community of women to grow up around and I can be my best self as she continues to grow.

I think any parent you ask would agree that their child's first year flies by and the tiny baby phase flies by without even realising because you're so caught up with work, family or just stress and worry.

But the main thing was, I was my best self, Jay had his business, was an amazing Father, we had our beautiful house and our parents were still living nearby, so we had that support system around us.

The next morning, we had Bellas nursery friends come over, along with some of our neighbours, Jays parents, Mom, Mike and Julie. We all enjoyed a little party, nothing too over the top, just some cake from Tesco, a few balloons and most of all, eachothers company.

After serving the cake, I sat outside on the front porch and thought to myself, "How lucky am I?" .... my beautiful baby girl was one, all my amazing family support us and love our girl just as much as we do and everything in life just felt right.

I am proud of what Jay & I have made together and built this future together, but I am also proud of myself, my individual achievements. I set out on this journey of self-discovery over 5 years ago, lost, scared, anxious, depressed you name it and I was feeling it! In the space of those 5 years, I have learned so much.

I learned how to deal with my emotions, good or bad, I learned about the importance of communication and not isolating yourself when something bad happens. How strong I really am, how my beliefs about myself were the only things holding me back from what I wanted in life. How creative I am, how beautiful my body is and how amazing it is to be able to grow my baby girl and go through a loss also.

I think the thing I took most, from all of this and my journey of Ruling Out The What Ifs, is, the What Ifs can easily be flipped around and looked at from a positive perspective.
For example, instead of thinking, "But what if it fails?" instead think "What if I succeed and its better than I ever could have hoped for!?"

Life is all about perspective.

As the saying goes... "If you ask for flowers, don't be surprised if it starts to rain".

Your journey, no matter how tough at the moment, is leading to something beautiful and only you, have the ability to rule out the what ifs and create the life you want and the life you deserve.

About the Author

I'm Robyn, a 22 year old woman from a little town called Cahersiveen in County Kerry, Ireland.

I have always had a passion for writing but it took a backseat as I tried to navigate my way through school and life in general.

I recently went through my own 'Quarter Life Crisis' and when I went looking for something to make me feel like I wasn't alone, I found nothing.

Eventually, #lifeinyour20s started trending on TikTok and I saw there were so many people feeling the same way. So I decided to take my passion for writing and make it into something that is relatable and something that can hopefully help at least one person realise Its okay to not have it all figured out by 25!

I am now living in Edinburgh, Scotland, which gave me the inspiration to base the book around my new local areas. I see my future in this beautiful city now and I hope to continue writing about various 'taboo' issues to bring awareness to the subjects and to realize life isn't all love and butterflies, but the hard parts are what makes us, who we are.

It's my turn to Rule out the What Ifs and see where my new career as an author can take me!

Love you and in case nobody has told you today, I'm proud of you x

Printed in Great Britain
by Amazon

46486664R00099